Finnegan's Farewell

An Interactive Musical Comedy Dinner Show

Conceived by Kevin Alexander

Created by Kevin Alexander and Chuck Santoro

A SAMUEL FRENCH ACTING EDITION

SAMUEL FRENCH

FOUNDED 1830

SAMUELFRENCH.COM
SAMUELFRENCH-LONDON.CO.UK

FINNEGAN'S FAREWELL was first produced by Joe Corcoran, production August 4, 1999 at St. Luke's Church in New York, New York. The production was directed by Chuck Santoro, with music supervision by Lynn Portas. The Dance Captain was Erin Pender. Costumes and hair were by Rosemary Keough, with flower arrangements by Randall Thropp. A casket, for us in the production, was provided by William Dengler Funeral Home, Summit, New Jersey. The Production Stage Manager was Ramona Spinelli-Mastrone, with assistance from Robert Kelly. The company Manager was Sean O'Brien. The cast was as follows:

PADDY FINNEGAN . . . . Tommy Carroll

MAGGIE FINNEGAN . . . . .Norma Crawford

PATRICK FINNEGAN . . . . Bart Shatto

ERIN FINNEGAN-GILBOY . . . . .Erin Pender

BRIAN FINNEGAN . . . . Tade Reen

COLLEEN FINNEGAN . . . . .Christine Siracusa

JIMMY GILBOY . . . . .Mark Aldrich

BROOKE LEWIS . . . . .Elizabeth Nagengast

BUSTY QUIVERS . . . . Sharon Angela

FATHER SEAMUS MCMURPHY . . . . Darren Dooley

BILL BUCKLEY . . . . Robert R. Oliver

KATHERINE BUCKLEY . . . . Katherine O'Sullivan

MAX GOLDSTEIN . . . . Roger Rifkin

TYRONE JEFFERSON . . . . .Shawn McLean

SWINGS . . . . Douglas Kampson, Martha Hawley

THE RIVER KIDS . . . . Bridget Geerlings, Meaghan Geerlings,
Siobhan Geerlings, Meaghan Ginnetty,
Kerry Hannigan

SWING KIDS . . . . .Meghan Allen, Shannon Geerlings

MUSICIANS

Marie Reilly . . . . Fiddle

John Geerlings . . . . .Keyboard

Martin Reilly . . . . Accordion

Robert Allen . . . . Bodhran

Terry McKee . . . . Bazuki

Frank Gleason . . . . Guitar

FINNEGAN'S FAREWELL was subsequently updated and revived at the Proctors Theater in Schenectady, New York on March 16, 2013. The production was directed by Chuck Santoro. The Production Manager was Tony Lauria. The cast was as follows:

PADDY FINNEGAN . . . . Richard Harte
MAGGIE FINNEGAN. . . . . Patricia Van Tassel
PATRICK FINNEGAN . . . . .Scott Raymond Johnson
BRIAN FINNEGAN . . . . Nick Muscatiello
ERIN FINNEGAN-GILBOY . . . . .Gretchen Dizer
COLLEEN FINNEGAN . . . . .Allison Mcardle
JIMMY GILBOY. . . . . .Paul Warren Smith
BRIDGET GILBOY . . . . Maggie McKeever, Gabriella Insero
KEVIN GILBOY. . . . . Nik Gatzendorfer
BROOKE LEWIS . . . . .Jen Thorpe Summersell
BUSTY QUIVERS. . . . . .Rebecca Douglas
FATHER SEAMUS MCMURPHY . . . . Patrick White
BILL BUCKLEY . . . . Kenneth Klapp
KATHRINE BUCKLEY. . . . . Susan Dantz
MAX GOLDSTEIN . . . . Raymond Kappes
TYRONE JEFFERSON . . . . .Dewitt Fleming Jr.
THE RIVER KIDS. . . . . Nora Stevens, Madeline Insero,
                                                Alyson Insero, Gabriella Insero,
                                             Maggie McKeever, Bailey Sawyer,
                                             Payton Sawyer
THE DUBLINEERS . . . . .Jordan Tirrell-Wysocki, Matt Jensen
BAGPIPER. . . . . Ally Crowley Duncan

CAST OF CHARACTERS

PADDY FINNEGAN – Family patriarch, postman, 60s

MAGGIE FINNEGAN – Family matriarch, lunch lady, 50

PATRICK FINNEGAN – Oldest son, FBI agent, 35

ERIN FINNEGAN-GILBOY – Oldest daughter, teacher, 32

BRIAN FINNEGAN – Youngest son, fireman, 25

COLLEEN FINNEGAN – Youngest daughter, waitress, 28

JIMMY GILBOY – Erin's husband, 35

BROOKE LEWIS – Patrick's fiancée, 30

BUSTY QUIVERS – Cocktail waitress, 35-40

FATHER SEAMUS MCMURPHY – Priest, 40s

BILL BUCKLEY – Mortician, 40s

KATHERINE BUCKLEY – Embalmer, 40s

MAX GOLDSTEIN – Lawyer, 40s

TYRONE JEFFERSON – Mailman, 20s

KEVIN GILBOY – Jimmy's younger brother, gay, dance teacher, 20s

BRIDGET GILBOY – Granddaughter, 5-9

THE RIVER KIDS – Irish Step Dancers, 5-16

THE DUBLINEERS – Irish Band

Character Biographies appear at the end of the script.

SPECIAL THANKS

Kevin Alexander and Chuck Santoro wish to thank the following people: Sean O'Brien, John and Maureen Geerlings, Susan Varon, Roger Rifkin, David Gersten, Liz Nagengast, Darren Dooley, James Hendricks, Ramona Spinelli-Mastrone, Marc Goldman, Amy Spiegel and Scott Fagant.

*For My Father
Alexander J. Leonidas
1917 – 2000*

ACT ONE

(Act One, exterior: outside Chapel.)

(As the mourners [the audience members] arrive, a bagpiper wearing a traditional kilt plays somber tunes. None of the selections that will be heard later at the service should be played now. As the door to the Chapel opens we hear a mix of traditional Irish laments and see chairs for the immediate family members, two upright candles and a table with a purple cloth draped over it with three prayer candles. Center stage is a podium.)

*(When the Chapel [the house] opens we see a woman in the fourth pew on house right sitting in the third seat from the aisle. She is dressed in black with accents of Zebra prints and a huge black hat. She is **BUSTY QUIVERS**, a slightly haggard but pretty cocktail waitress from [any local town, not the greatest]. She has arrived early. Outside the entrance of the Chapel is **BILL BUCKLEY**, the mortician and his wife, **KATHERINE BUCKLEY**, the embalmer. They greet and welcome the mourners.)*

*(**KATHERINE** and **BILL** have put together a display of Finnegan family photographs. The display of framed photographs should be of the past and present: **PADDY**'s baby picture, **PADDY** as a youth in Ireland, **PADDY** and **MAGGIE** on their honeymoon. Also included on the table are photographs of **BRIAN**, **PATRICK**, **ERIN** and **COLLEEN**. There should be a shot of **BRIAN** playing sports as well as **PATRICK** and **BROOKE**'s engagement photo.)*

*(The first to arrive outside is **BRIAN FINNEGAN**, the youngest son who is in his fireman's uniform. He is smoking and stays outside the Chapel as he greets the*

mourners [the audience members]. He is waiting for his brother **PATRICK FINNEGAN** *who is coming from Washington, DC and is late.* **BRIAN** *is blaming* **PATRICK**'s *tardiness on* **PATRICK**'s *fiancée* **BROOKE LEWIS**, *who is not one of* **BRIAN**'s *favorite people. As he is waiting for all of the family members to arrive he finds some time to flirt with most of the women in attendance.* **BRIAN** *should pick out an audience member to be a pallbearer.)*

*(***FATHER SEAMUS MCMURPHY** *arrives next. He gives his condolences to* **BRIAN** *and some of the other mourners. He goes inside the Chapel. Once inside he takes his time greeting the congregation.)*

*(***FATHER SEAMUS** *then goes to where the family members have gathered in a receiving line to greet the incoming guests. When he's finished, he goes up on the altar to light the candles. He exits into the vestibule where he will put on his religious stole and vestments.)*

(The next to arrive are **ERIN** *and her husband* **JIMMY GILBOY, KEVIN GILBOY. KEVIN** *is carrying* **BRIDGET**'s *trophy. They are late because they waited for* **PATRICK** *and* **BROOKE** *to show up.* **PATRICK** *was supposed to arrive at* **ERIN**'s *house 10 minutes from where the service is [pick a local town with a high Irish population] but he never showed.* **ERIN** *maintains a stoic demeanor; she is not a person who shows her emotions. It takes a lot to ruffle her feathers.* **ERIN** *is a perfectionist to the umpteenth degree. She has planned the entire funeral and knows where every penny has and will be spent. It's like her checkbook. She is a control freak and wants things her way or no way at all.)*

*(***ERIN** *tells* **BRIAN** *that her daughter* **BRIDGET** *will perform an Irish step dance number with her fellow classmates as a memorial tribute to her late father.* **JIMMY** *goes into the Chapel to help* **BRIAN** *with the seating.* **ERIN, JIMMY, KEVIN** *stand in the receiving line and greet the guests.)*

*(Next we see **MAX GOLDSTEIN**, the Finnegan family attorney and friend. He has just come from his office, which is located down the street. He is carrying his shoddy briefcase and his pocket is filled with his business cards, which he will hand out to prospective clients. He greets **ERIN** and **BRIAN** and informs them that **PADDY** had requested that his will be read at the wake. **ERIN** is angry that she wasn't notified about the reading of the will. **MAX** informs her that the only person who knew about this was her mother. **ERIN** makes it known to **MAX** and **BRIAN** that she thinks it would be tasteless and inappropriate to read the will. She leaves in a huff and exists into the Chapel. **MAX** enters and introduces himself to the guests with his business cards in hand.)*

*(The next to arrive is **TYRONE JEFFERSON**, a co-worker of **PADDY**'s from the Post Office. He is wearing his postal uniform. He greets **BRIAN** and gives him a hug. **BRIAN** asks **TYRONE** to be a pallbearer. He goes into the Chapel and greets the others. After **TYRONE** is finished greeting guests in the receiving line, He sits in a seat on the left aisle.)*

*(**TYRONE** places his hat and sweater on the seat and then he goes around the room introducing himself to the others in attendance. **ERIN** is upset about the reading of the will. She goes to **JIMMY** and informs him of this. **JIMMY** tries to calm her down. **ERIN** wants to know who the pallbearers will be. **BRIAN** tells her that it will be himself, **PATRICK**, **JIMMY**, **TYRONE** and two of dad's "friends" [audience members].)*

*(She has no problem letting **BRIAN** know that **TYRONE** is an unacceptable choice. She blames it on the fact that he is not an immediate family member. She states that "He's not even Irish!" next to arrive are **PATRICK FINNEGAN** and his fiancée **BROOKE LEWIS**. They are arguing while she is applying last minute touch-ups to her face. **PATRICK** hugs **BRIAN**. **BROOKE** quickly extends her hand for him to kiss; she doesn't want him to*

muss her makeup. **BRIAN** *knows this, but he gives her a big sloppy wet kiss anyway. While* **BROOKE** *is reapplying her makeup,* **BRIAN** *warns* **PATRICK** *to stay clear of their sister* **ERIN**. **BRIAN** *tells him she is upset about a number of things.* **PATRICK** *says, "like what?"* **BRIAN** *lists them: the reading of the will, him being late,* **MAGGIE**'s *forgetfulness,* **TYRONE** *being a pallbearer.* **PATRICK** *says sarcastically, "is that all?")*

*(***PATRICK** *and* **BROOKE** *enter the Chapel.* **ERIN** *sees* **BROOKE** *and* **PATRICK** *enter.* **ERIN** *tries desperately to put on a happy face. She goes to give* **BROOKE** *a kiss on the cheek, but* **BROOKE** *puts her hand out instead.)*

*(***BROOKE** *apologizes to her for being late. She blames it on the traffic.* **PATRICK** *greets* **JIMMY***; they have a mutual fondness for one another. They have much in common. They understand that they have both chosen women who are a handful, to say the least.* **BROOKE** *goes to* **JIMMY** *and greets him, while* **PATRICK** *hugs* **ERIN**. **ERIN** *warmly hugs him, but in reality she is seething with anger. She tries not to show it, but it is apparent in her gestures, which are quick and abrupt.* **PATRICK** *finds a seat for* **BROOKE** *in the first row.* **BROOKE** *complains to* **PATRICK** *about the tackiness of the Chapel décor. She's upset that the seats are not cushioned. She takes out a handkerchief and cleans off her seat.)*

*(***MAGGIE FINNEGAN** *arrives and is accompanied by her granddaughter* **BRIDGET**. **MAGGIE** *is greeted by her son,* **BRIAN**. *She greets the bagpiper and thanks him for his services. She greets the mourners with hugs and kisses. Then she proceeds to enter the Chapel.* **MAGGIE** *greets* **BILL** *and* **KATHERINE**, *who are standing next to the table with photographs of the family. She scrutinizes each photo as if she were general doing a uniform inspection of her troops. She has a story or comment for each one. It's like a show and tell moment for her and any of the lucky mourners that happen to pass the table.* **MAGGIE** *joins the receiving line to greet the guests.)*

*(She then goes outside to retrieve the bagpiper and inform him that he will the lead the procession up the Chapel aisle. She thanks **KATHERINE** and **BILL** for all their work and asks them if the mourners have arrived. **KATHERINE** tells her no, but she is sure she could find some. She and **BILL** go into crowd and ask 4 to 6 audience members if they could be mourners to honor **PADDY**. They tell them all they need to do is cry and wail, very loudly. They give them all black veils. **BRIAN** and **PATRICK** locate the men who've been asked to be pallbearers, he gives them black armbands. They also get **TYRONE** up as well. **KATHERINE** and **BILL** have readied the casket and everyone is in their places. As the doors reopen, we hear the bagpiper. He is playing, "Scotland The Brave." **FATHER SEAMUS** enters. He crosses to the altar.)*

FATHER SEAMUS. Will the congregation please rise.

*(The bagpiper leads off the procession. He is followed by two altar girls who are holding lit prayer candles. Then the mourners in their black veils. Behind them is the casket. Surrounding the casket are six men. **BRIAN** and **PATRICK** are at the head of the casket, followed by the two audience members in the middle and **TYRONE** and **JIMMY** at the end. Each man holds onto the casket as it is wheeled down the aisle. Directly behind them are **MAGGIE** and **ERIN**. **MAGGIE** is weeping uncontrollably as she is escorted by a teary-eyed **ERIN**. **ERIN** is trying to console her mother. **KEVIN GILBOY** follows behind with a flower piece in the shape of a Shamrock. The two altar girls proceed to the altar and place the candles into the upright candle holders at each end of the altar. They then go to their seats which are at the opposite ends of the altar and they stand in place.)*

*(Once the procession reaches the altar, the men position the casket horizontally to the altar. The family takes seats on the altar. There are six chairs, three on each side. **MAGGIE** sits in the seat closest to the podium. **ERIN***

is seated next to her. The seat closest to the audience is currently empty.)

(Across from them are three chairs. **PATRICK** *is in the middle chair and* **BRIAN** *is seated closest to the audience. The upstage chair is empty.* **TYRONE** *and* **JIMMY** *go to their seats in the audience. The bagpiper finishes his tune, then exits.* **BILL** *and* **KATHERINE** *close the doors.)*

*(***FATHER SEAMUS*** begins to address the congregation.)*

FATHER SEAMUS. Please be seated *(The audience sits down.)* We pray. O Lord how long will you utterly forget me? How long will you hide your face from me? How long should I harbor sorrow in my soul; grief in my heart day after day. How long will my enemy triumph over me? Lord, answer me, and hear my call…

(He gets cut off by the sound of a ringing cell phone. **BROOKE** *stands up and looks around, She tries to dash out but she is too embarrassed. She answers the phone.)*

BROOKE. Hello hello? They hung up. I'm so sorry, It was my acupuncturist. Bad service. So sorry father.

*(***FATHER SEAMUS*** is slightly annoyed by this disturbance, but tries not to show it. He proceeds again with the prayer.)*

FATHER SEAMUS. Really? Can we please turn off all electronics, noise making devices and cell phones. Thank you. Dearly beloved, we are gathered here to say goodbye to a great man, Patrick James Finnegan. A caring father to his two sons, Patrick and Brian, and his two beautiful daughters, Erin and Colleen. Colleen, I understand, is living in California and will not be with us today. And let us not forget the other family members, Erin's husband Jimmy Gilboy, Paddy's granddaughter Bridget, and Patrick's lovely fiancée Brooke. Paddy was a man whose heart was filled with nothing but love for his fellow man. He never took things for granted and always thanked God for the many good things that had come his way. He'd always be telling people that he wished God had given him more than ten fingers, so that could count his many blessings. I remember when he won all that money at the Casino last year. I'm not quite sure but I think it was over a million dollars...

(**MAX** *interrupts the priest.*)

MAX. *(aside to the people next to him)* It was a hell of a lot more than that.

FATHER SEAMUS. Pardon me?

MAX. Excuse me Father. *(He stands up and turns to the crowd.)* May I interject a moment? My name is Max Goldstein, Esquire. I represent the late Mr. Finnegan. May I approach the bench?

FATHER SEAMUS. This is not a bench.

(**FATHER SEAMUS** *looks at* **MAX** *as if he has two heads.*)

MAX. Can we speak? I don't mean to be pedantic but the will clearly states that it was 2.2 million.

FATHER SEAMUS. Thank you Mr. Goldstein.

MAX. I apologize if I'm a little out of place. My people usually just sit "shiva."

FATHER SEAMUS. Thank you again. I think we could move on, wouldn't you?

MAX. Yes of course.

(He starts to walk back to his chair. In a loud whisper he asks the person seated next to him:)

Did he just call me a "wooden jew"?

(**MAX** *sits down.*)

FATHER SEAMUS. As Mr. Goldenstein was so thoughtful to point out, it was 2.2 million. In fact, he made more money the minute he pulled that handle on that slot machine than made in his entire twenty-five years of service at the United States Post Office. He came to me at the rectory. "Father Seamus," he said, "I worry that winning all this money is going to change my life forever." I told him that the only thing that will change for sure is your bank account. Remember that, "A heavenly changed change purse changes a heavy purse into a light heart." And because you have God's strength and his blessing, you will never be tempted to stray from his holy path. But, unfortunately, he's taken that road a little earlier than expected.

(**MAGGIE** *starts to cry.*)

And we must never forget that it is just as hard for a rich man to enter the kingdom of heaven as it is for a poor man to get out of *[name local town]*. You know, Paddy was thinking about retiring after he won all that money, be he quickly changed his mind, because he realized that he loved his job more than life itself. Well Paddy, that fall from the ladder was no accident at all. As the great philosopher Kierkegaard might have said, "It's God's way of saying it's time, time for a new ladder." I believe that we will be hearing from Paddy's oldest son, Patrick.

(**PATRICK FINNEGAN** *stands up and goes to the podium.* **FATHER SEAMUS** *steps back and stands behind* **MAGGIE.**)

PATRICK. Thank you Father Seamus. I'd like to start off by saying that the last thing my father would want to see is his friends and family mourning his passing. Instead let us celebrate his life. The life of a good man, devoted husband, father, grandfather and friend. I remember when I was a kid and he helped coach our little league team. We had a terrible team

BRIAN. Yeah, one loss after the other.

PATRICK. Thanks Brian. But if you remember the next season he whipped us into shape by going back to the basics of the game. He'd always start off practice by saying, "Boys remember, he who climbs the ladder must begin at the bottom." Well that and a little Irish luck brought us the championship. I began my career in government as an intern in Washington.

Thank you. I currently work for the Federal Bureau of Investigation. Most of the time I'm asked to put my work above all else, something of which I think I learned from my Dad. My beautiful fiancée Brooke can attest to that. Through the years I've climbed that ladder of public service, like Dad, with honor and integrity. I never would have gotten as far as I have without the determination and confidence that was instilled in me by my father.

(**FATHER SEAMUS** *walks over to shake* **PATRICK**'s *hand.*)

FATHER SEAMUS. Thank you Patrick.

(**PATRICK** *is lost in his own world and doesn't notice the priest. Obviously he is not finished.*)

PATRICK. I'd like to sing a song for him now, the same one he used to sing me as a child.

(**PATRICK** *sings the first few verses of "Danny Boy" very somberly.*)

O DANNY BOY,
THE PIPES THE PIPES ARE CALLING,
FROM GLEN TO GLEN AND DOWN THE MOUNTAIN SIDE.
THE SUMMER'S GONE AND ALL THE ROSES FALLING,
IT'S YOU IT'S YOU
MUST GO AND I MUST BIDE.

BUT COME YE BACK,
WHEN SUMMER'S IN THE MEADOW,
OR WHEN THE VALLEY'S HUSHED AND WHITE WITH SNOW.
'TIS I'LL BE HERE IN THE SUNSHINE OR IN SHADOW.
OH DANNY BOY,
OH DANNY BOY I LOVE YOU SO.

(*It appears that he has finished singing, but then it's as if the Holy Spirit has entered his body. He turns "Danny Boy" into an over-the-top show stopper.*)

BUT...
WHEN YE COME AND ALL THE FLOWERS ARE DYING,
IF I AM DEAD,

AS DEAD I WELL MAY BE,
YE'LL COME AND FIND THE PLACE WHERE I AM LYING,
AND KNEEL AND SAY AND AVE THERE FOR ME

(*While* **PATRICK** *takes a brief pause for a breath,* **MAGGIE** *speaks.*)

MAGGIE. Patrick what are you doing?

(**PATRICK** *doesn't hear* **MAGGIE**. *He continues to sing his heart out.*)

PATRICK.

AND I SHALL HEAR,
THROUGH SOFT YOU TREAD ABOVE ME,
AND ALL MY GRAVE WILL WARMER,
SWEETER BE.
FOR YOU WILL BEND AND TELL ME THAT YOU LOVE ME,
AND I SHALL SLEEP IN PEACE UNTIL YOU COME TO

(*He takes a big breath.*)

ME!!!!!!

(**PATRICK** *finishes the song. He is numb to what has just happened.* **BRIAN** *gives him a bear hug. They both sit down.* **FATHER SEAMUS** *goes to the podium.*)

FATHER SEAMUS. Thank you Patrick. Unfortunately we're a little behind so there's no need for an encore. But I'm sure Paddy's smiling from here to Killarney after hearing that rendition. Now I'd like to call upon Paddy's youngest son, Brian. (**FATHER SEAMUS** *turns to* **MAGGIE** *and in a loud hush:*) He's not going to sing too, is he?

(**MAGGIE** *shakes her head emphatically no.*)

(**BRIAN** *stands up and goes to the podium. He leans on it with his elbows.*)

BRIAN. Hey, everybody what's up? I just wanted to thank everybody for all the cards, phone calls, fruit baskets and all the other shit.

(**BRIAN** *suddenly realizes he cursed. He is embarrassed.* **FATHER SEAMUS** *gives him a look of disapproval.* **BRIAN** *apologizes and continues.*)

Sorry Father, all the other "stuff" that we received this week. I especially want to thank all the guys from the firehouse, Rob, Tommy Boy and Stinky. *(He points to three audience members.)* Thanks guys. We all know how much Pop loved being surrounded by his family and friends. Whether he was sitting in O'Leary's Pub with a pint of beer that someone probably bought for him, or stopping by the track to place a bet or get a tip on a horse from his pal Denny the mush, Mom would always say, *(He imitates her:)* "If you spotted his mail cart, you knew he was only a few feet away."

(**MAGGIE** *interrupts him, she is angry at* **BRIAN** *for embarrassing her.*)

MAGGIE. I don't sound like that do I?

BRIAN. No, not at all Mom.

(**BRIAN** *rolls his eyes at the audience. He gives a look to* **PATRICK** *as if we know who's really telling the truth.*)

Well Dad, I know where that mail cart is right now. It's right outside the pearly gates and I know that you're sitting right next to God just a few feet away. (**BRIAN** *takes a moment to compose himself.*) After the service, our family would like to invite everyone to stay for a little dinner and some drinks. That's what Dad would of wanted. Thank you.

(He sits down.)

(**FATHER SEAMUS** *steps back to the podium.*)

FATHER SEAMUS. Thank you Brian. Thank you for being you. As that great Irishman George Bernard Shaw once said, "Life does not cease to be funny when someone dies anymore than ceases to be serious when someone laughs."

(**BRIAN** *tries desperately to comprehend what was just said, bit goes right over his head.* **BRIAN** *asks* **PATRICK** *to explain the quote to him.*)

Right now I'd like to introduce Paddy's oldest daughter, Erin.

ERIN. Thank you Father Seamus. As most of you already know, I teach the seventh grade class at Our Lady of Visitation in *[local town]*. Dad would always tell me how much he loved my voice.

(*She shoots* **PATRICK** *a look of venom.*)

And it's a little known fact that each and every morning after the children and I say morning prayers, we begin the school day by raising our voices in "Amazing Grace." (*She steps in front of the podium.*) So I would like us all to sing the chorus and I'll sing the verses all by myself.

(**ERIN** *steps off the altar and stands in front of the casket. During the song, she walks up and down the aisle as if she is monitoring her students during an exam. She gently encourages them to sing, suggesting throughout the song,* "Sit up straight," "You sound beautiful," "You're a little flat," *etc.*)

ERIN & CONGREGATION.
AMAZING GRACE HOW SWEET THE SOUND,
THAT SAVED A WRETCH LIKE ME.
I ONCE WAS LOST BUT NOW AM FOUND,
WAS BLIND BUT NOW I SEE.

ERIN.
T'WAS GRACE THAT TAUGHT MY HEART TO FEAR AND
GRACE MY FEARS RELIEVED.
HOW PRECIOUS DID THAT GRACE APPEAR THAT HOUR I
FIRST BELIEVED.

(*She spins around, arms outstretched in the air and speaks:*)

Everybody!

ERIN & CONGREGATION.
> AMAZING GRACE HOW SWEET THE SOUND,
> THAT SAVED A WRETCH LIKE ME.
>
> *(ERIN speaks on pitch:)* I can't hear you.
>
> I ONCE WAS LOST BUT NOW AM FOUND,
> WAS BLIND BUT NOW I SEE.
>
> *(ERIN sings solo again, walking toward the casket.)*

ERIN.
> THROUGH MANY DANGERS,
> TOILS AND SNARES,
> I HAVE ALREADY COME
>
> *(COLLEEN has entered from the back of the Chapel. She has just flown in from the coast and is wheeling her luggage behind her. ERIN has her back to COLLEEN and doesn't notice that her sister has entered. PATRICK stands up and shouts.)*

PATRICK. Colleen!

> *(Everyone stops singing. ERIN turns around to see her long lost sister. As if she were a deer in headlights, ERIN is speechless. COLLEEN starts to applaud her sister very deliberately.)*

ERIN. Well, if it isn't the prodigal daughter?

COLLEEN. Oh I'm sorry. I thought that I was coming to my father's funeral, not a recital.

ERIN. I'm not the one making the dramatic entrance.

COLLEEN. I see nothing has changed. I don't have to listen to this.

> *(MAGGIE gets up and walks down to greet COLLEEN before things get heated between the siblings.)*

ERIN. Oh really Colleen? The only time you listen is when money talks.

> *(ERIN starts to approach COLLEEN but is abruptly stopped when MAGGIE steps between them.)*

MAGGIE. Erin stop that!

(**MAGGIE** *hugs* **COLLEEN**.)

Oh Colleen, we missed you so much. Come, bring your suitcase with you and sit with us.

(**MAGGIE** *takes* **COLLEEN** *by the hand and walks her up the aisle, pushing* **ERIN** *out of the way.*)

Erin get out of the way!

(**ERIN** *walks back up the aisle, she looks at the casket and says:*)

ERIN. Sheeee's back!

(**MAGGIE** *brings* **COLLEEN** *up to the altar. She tells her to sit next to her.* **ERIN** *complains to* **JIMMY**.)

She's sitting in my seat. I'm supposed to sit next to Mom.

(**MAGGIE** *has* **COLLEEN** *sit in* **ERIN**'s *seat.* **ERIN** *goes to pull her sister out of the chair, but* **PATRICK** *quickly grabs her and whisks her to the boys' side of seats. He tells her to sit in the chair next to him.* **ERIN** *is very upset. Things are not in her control.*)

FATHER SEAMUS. I know this is a difficult time for all of us. Like the lost sheep, let us welcome Colleen back into the fold. The fold of our family, the family of God. Lest we keep in mind, to quote Bob Villa, "a house divided against itself cannot stand."

(**FATHER SEAMUS** *slams his hand on the podium.* **BRIAN** *is trying to calm* **ERIN**'s *nerves and is not paying attention to* **FATHER SEAMUS**, *but when he hears the word "stand," he gets up. Being the good Catholic boy that he is, he goes on automatic pilot when in church.* **FATHER SEAMUS** *motions him to sit down.* **BRIAN** *is thoroughly embarrassed.*)

Now I'd like to share one of my favorite quotes from "Oprah"...

(**MAGGIE** *cuts him off.*)

MAGGIE. Thank you Father Seamus. I think I should say something too. *(She stands up and makes her way to the podium.)* As I look out and see all your faces, I just know my late husband would be overjoyed to see so many people here. The United States Post Office lost their best worker.

*(She directs her question to **TYRONE**.)*

Isn't that right Tyrone?

*(**TYRONE** stands.)*

TYRONE. Yes ma'am, Mrs. Finnegan. Neither snow nor rain, or sleet or hell and highwater!

BRIAN. Go Postal! *(**BRIAN** raises his fist in support for **TYRONE**)*

(He sits down.)

MAGGIE. Thank you Tyrone. Anyway as I was saying, Paddy was a good man, a happy man and, by the size of the crowd, a man who was loved by everyone.

*(We hear a loud cry. It's **BUSTY QUIVERS**. She is very distraught. As she makes her way down the aisle, she's blowing her nose and crying simultaneously, she goes to the casket and starts to caress and rub her body on it. Then she runs out the door. Everyone turns their head at the same time to **MAGGIE**.)*

Who was that? Paddy must of touched her deeply.

*(**BRIAN** makes a suggestion that it was more.)*

*(**MAGGIE** wonders who this mysterious woman could be. **MAGGIE** does a quick reality check, but she dismisses the thought that her husband could have been an adulterer.)*

Anyway, Paddy always wanted to celebrate our good fortune with our family and friends. So he planned a huge party. But I wasn't about to have anyone over, the place was a mess. We were still living like shanty Irish. And I didn't enjoy the neighbors referring to us as the "Clampets," either. I told him, "if I'm a millionaire, I want to start living like one. I want the place painted, wall to wall carpeting, and some of that new fancy eye-talian furniture." But Paddy decided to paint the place himself. And that's when I found him, lying on his back, a paintbrush in one hand and an empty whiskey bottle in the other. I begged him to let someone else do the job. But you know Paddy, he always had low pockets and short arms. I loved him and I'll miss him terribly.

(**MAGGIE** *starts to sob. She's a mess.*)

Oh Paddy! Oh he's gone! What am I going to do?

(*She runs to the casket and throws herself on it.*)

I want to see him, just one more time. Once more! Please!

(*The family runs to her aid.* **PATRICK** *and* **BRIAN** *try to pry her off the casket, but she won't let it go. They pull her off and back into her seat.*)

FATHER SEAMUS. Now there, Maggie. We must know that it is okay to cry. Because it's God's will and after all, there's no good crying when the funeral's over.

MAGGIE. I think we would all like to see him resting so comfortably in his place. If no one minds, we'd like to open the casket.

(*Everyone looks to the rear where* **BILL** *is standing.* **BILL** *doesn't move.*)

Open it!

FATHER SEAMUS. Very well then. Can we get cousin Bill the mortician and his wife Katherine the embalmer up here to open the casket?

(**KATHERINE** *pushes* **BILL** *down the aisle. He is startled.*)

BILL. I don't think it would be right.

(**KATHERINE** *pushes him further down the aisle.*)

MAX. (*stands up.*) I object!

FATHER SEAMUS. Overruled! Sit down.

BILL. I can't. I'm too scared.

(**BILL** *is trembling.* **KATHERINE** *pushes* **BILL** *forward towards the front of the altar.* **BILL** *winds up at the head of the casket.* **KATHERINE** *is at the foot end of the casket.*)

KATHERINE. You'll have to excuse him, the dead ones give him the hebie jebies.

(**KATHERINE** *and* **BILL** *are now at each end of the casket.* **BILL** *is trembling. He is staring out at the crowd; his eyes are crossed and he shakes with fear.* **KATHERINE** *motions to her husband to open the casket. He is frozen in fear. She startles him by stomping her foot on the floor.*)

Open it you eigot[*]!

(*Before he opens it, the family has gathered around to witness the event. They are standing on the altar directly above the casket. As the casket lid is opened,* **MAGGIE** *lets out a scream. Everyone is horrified at the view of an empty casket.*)

MAGGIE. Oh my God. It's empty!

(*She faints into her chair.* **ERIN** *and* **JIMMY** *run to help her. The next sequence of speeches should move very quickly, sometimes overlapping each other.*)

FATHER SEAMUS. What in God's name is going on here?

BILL. There seems to have been a mix up at the funeral home.

PATRICK. Where the hell is my father?

KATHERINE. Yeah, where the hell is his father?

BILL. I think he's in *[town 30 minutes away]*.

BRIAN. *[town 30 minutes away]*?

COLLEEN. He hates *[town 30 minutes away]*!

MAX. We'll sue the schmuck!

BROOKE. What's a schmuck?

BRIAN. Let me have a piece of him.

---

[*] Her heavy brogue turns the word idiot into sounding like E-jet.

(**BRIAN** *grabs* **BILL** *and lifts him up over his shoulders. He starts to carry him out.* **TYRONE** *stands up and cheers for a possible fight to occur.*)

(**MAGGIE** *walks down and stands in front of the casket.*)

MAGGIE. Stop it! (*She stampedes down to* **BRIAN** *and* **BILL***.*) Brian, put him down, right now! I'm going to put an end to this craziness right now. Bill? I don't care how you do it, but you find my husband's body. And bring it and your skinny little arse back here. And if you're not back by the time we finish dinner the three of you will be hanging from the chandelier!

BILL. The three of us?

MAGGIE. Yes. You and your two little balls. (*She points to him, then to his crotch.*) Now get going!

(**BILL** *runs down the aisle and exits.* **KATHERINE** *chases him off and is muttering something Gaelic.* **MAGGIE** *returns to the casket and closes the lid.* **BRIAN** *returns to the family members who have been watching from the altar.*)

FATHER SEAMUS. I think we should be confident that they will find poor Paddy's body for balls (*corrects himself:*) Bill's sake, so that we can give him the proper burial that he deserves. Lest we not forget that we can still mourn without having a body present. After all, it's merely just a corpse, if you will. Or as the great peanut farmer George W. Carver once said, "All that is left is an empty shell, the nut missing." I'd like to conclude our services with an old Irish blessing.

(*Everyone bows their heads except* **MAGGIE***. She is still trying to figure out this situation. She is very confused. Her wheels are spinning.*)

May the road rise up to meet you. May the wind be always at your back. May the sun shine warm upon your face. Until we meet again, may God hold you in the palm of his hand and not squeeze too tightly. Amen. In the name of the Father, the Son and the Holy Spirit. Go in peace.

(**MAGGIE** *is upset and infuriated. She storms down the aisle and out, escorted by* **COLLEEN**.*)*

MAGGIE. Jesus, Mary and Joseph. What the hell is going on here?

(**FATHER SEAMUS** *follows behind them. The men,* **TYRONE, BRIAN, PATRICK** *and* **JIMMY**, *prepare to take the casket down the aisle in the same formation that they entered, excluding the two audience members.* **ERIN** *grabs* **BRIDGET** *and exits down the aisle.* **BROOKE** *is following them, showing no emotion at all, just annoyance that she has to be here at all.)*

(**MAX** *gets up on the altar to make an announcement. The band starts to set up behind him and the lighting starts to change)*

MAX. Ladies and Gentleman, If I can have your attention for just a moment. As you know Paddy has left some money for his family and friends for a little nosh at his wake. And I have to say they have some spread coming your way! No Matzoh Ball soup, but I'll live. I have to say I am a little upset with the dessert, no ice cream sad to say. Paddy and I loved ice cream. Did you know that Ben and Jerry's Ice Cream is now available in Israel? It's true. In the following flavors: Wailing Walnut, Moishemellow. and my personal favorite, Mazel Toffee!

So try and enjoy yourself, remember our old friend Paddy and hopefully we'll be able to read the will sometime between now and Hanukkah.

(If you are not moving rooms, then he would say the following, if changing rooms cut the following line)

Ok now lets play some music. A little song and little dance a little seltzer down your pants. Just kidding. It's what our friend Paddy would have wanted!

End of Act One

ACT TWO

(The band starts to play some upbeat Irish music. **BRIAN** *starts to get some audience members up and dancing.* **PATRICK, BRIAN** *and* **JIMMY** *are placing the casket near the Bandstand.* **KATHERINE** *follows closely behind with the flower arrangement for the top of the casket, and* **KEVIN** *with the Shamrock arrangement. She also will set up all the family pictures and mass cards on a table in the entrance of the hall.)*

*(***MAGGIE** *with* **COLLEEN** *finds their way to the Finnegan family table, which is positioned off the dance floor, house right.* **FATHER SEAMUS** *goes to the bar and asks for a drink.* **BROOKE,** *who has been told that her table is in the back near the smoking area, is not happy with the seat she was given and demands to be moved to another location. After the boys have moved the casket,* **PATRICK** *goes to* **BROOKE** *and tries to calm her down.)*

*(***JIMMY** *seats the remaining guests.* **BRIAN** *goes to the bar and gets a beer and finds* **COLEEN** *who he takes on the dance floor.* **TYRONE** *finds a seat in the audience.)*

*(***MAGGIE** *crosses from the table to the casket to make sure everything looks alright with* **KATHERINE.** *)*

*(***BUSTY** *is the last to enter. She sits at a table on the edge of the dance floor house left. She realizes she can't smoke at her table and crosses back to the bar to have a cigarette, if no smoking is allowed she takes out an e-cigarette.)*

(Once the audience is seated and the cast members have taken their places around the room, **PATRICK** *crosses to the center of the Bandstand and starts to speak into the microphone.)*

PATRICK. Let's hear it for the Dublineers, Declan O'Mally and Will Dew *[or the real names of the musicians on stage]* who came all the way from Donegal to be with us today! Actually we were just lucky that the Irish Pub down the street closed down due to health inspection violations, and these guys were stuck in town but we are thrilled to have them. If I can have your attention for just a minute, I'd like to welcome everyone and introduce to you my brother-in-law who happens to be the manager around here. Come on up here, Jimmy Gilboy.

(**JIMMY** *takes the microphone from* **PATRICK.**)

JIMMY. Thank you Patrick. I'd like to welcome all of you. As requested by Paddy, he wanted us to have a good old time with some of the money he left behind. So we're going to celebrate with good food, foot-stomping Irish music and great dancing. I got a little note that Paddy left for us to read if this day was ever to come. It says, "To all my friends I'm leaving a little extra dough for a party at my wake. So everything's on the house, except the drinks." But before we open up the buffet, my wife Erin has an announcement.

(**ERIN**, *who has been sitting at the Finnegan family table, crosses to the microphone.*)

ERIN. As most of you have heard, my daughter Bridget won her first Irish dancing competition at the *[name of state]* Irish Arts Festival last weekend. Thank you, thank you. She's made me one very proud mommy. She's a natural, and I'm sure that one day she'll even outshine me!

(**BRIAN** *is standing at the bar with* **COLLEEN**. *He shouts.*)

BRIAN. Bridget, you better pray that day never comes!

COLLEEN. Yeah, she'll kill the kid!

ERIN. Ladies and gentlemen, I present to you my daughter Bridget, my brother in law and her teacher Kevin Gilboy, and the River Kids!

*(The **RIVER KIDS** do a slip jig. **KEVIN** is calling out certain moves to them and far front performing some of the moves himself. **ERIN** is brimming with glee)*

KEVIN. Higher Meghan!!! *(coaching the girls:)* Big Smile Shannon. More teeth. *(He turns to an audience member.)* You don't see that at [a rival town] Irish Arts Academy!

*(He at some point crosses to **BRIDGET** to fix her costume and straighten her hair. Erin encourages the audience to cheer. **COLLEEN** is nauseated by **ERIN**'s flagrant attempt to showcase her child. **COLLEEN** complains to anyone at the bar who will listen to her.)*

JIMMY. *(as the dance ends and the children exit:)* Let's hear it for the River Kids and my brother Kevin!

*(**KEVIN** does a grand jeté and bows very dramatically)*

I would now like to call Father Seamus up to say a blessing.

*(**FATHER SEAMUS** crosses to the Bandstand and takes the microphone.)*

FATHER SEAMUS. Like the goodness of the five loaves and the fishes, which God divided among the five thousand men, may the blessing of the King who so divided be upon our share of this common meal.

*(As he finishes the prayer, he is interrupted by shouting from the back of the room. It's **BILL**. He runs down the center aisle, and shouts.)*

BILL. Father Seamus, Father Seamus! I've got good news! *(**BILL** goes to the microphone.)* Everybody listen up. I've got great news. I found Paddy's body. It was mistakenly shipped to the Corcoran Brothers Funeral Home in [town 30 minutes way]. Don't worry, cause my driver has an EZ pass [or the other highway toll system]. They'll be here soon.

JIMMY. Alright I know all of you are hungry, so in honor of Paddy we have prepared a traditional seven course Irish Meal: a six pack and a potato. Only kidding. *[He announces what the actual meal will be.]* As Erin calls you up, table by table, please form two lines. Grab a plate, fork and enjoy the music of the Dublineers.

(Dinner can be a buffet, family style or plated service.)

*(**KATHERINE** goes to tables showing everyone her catalogue of caskets as well as handing out some business cards.)*

*(**BRIAN** offers to buy **FATHER SEAMUS** a drink. He resists at first, but after some convincing he accepts.)*

*(**MAX**, who loves a free meal, stacks his plate with extra helpings of everything in sight and sits wherever there is an empty seat with the mourners.)*

*(**BROOKE** is irritated that she can't get good reception on her cell phone and shakes it. She tells **PATRICK** that she forgot to feed the dogs, Skye and Lark and she wants to drive back home right now. While the two of them argue **MAGGIE** comes over and sees that neither one has gotten any food. **MAGGIE** crosses to the front of the buffet line and gets two plates for them. When she presents the full plates to them she is greeted by resistance from **BROOKE**, who is not happy with the food being served and asks if a Gluten free option is available.)*

*(After two traditional Irish Songs, **BRIAN** comes on stage with a few male audience members.)*

BRIAN. So my father and I went to Boston a few months ago to catch a Celtics game and heard this song and he loved it! Dad this ones for you.

*(The band plays a lively song about going off to Boston and **BRIAN** and the men sing the chorus)*

*(**TYRONE** spots **COLLEEN** at the bar and crosses to her. The two sit at the table in the front of the bar at the back*

of the house. While **ERIN** *is calling each table up to eat, she notices the two of them talking and is disgusted with the situation.)*

(The bagpiper now comes to the stage, introduced by the lead singer of the band and plays a nontraditional song on the pipes accompanied by the Dublineers. The tune should be something very pop and recognizable but nothing you would normally hear on a bagpipe.)

*(***FATHER SEAMUS** *decides to have just one more drink. He figures he can let loose a little bit now that the Chapel service is over. He starts to get a warm fuzzy feeling from the spirits and starts to entertain the bartender and some of the people at the bar with an old Irish ditty. He starts singing.* **BUSTY***, who is too "distraught with grief to eat," goes to the bar for a drink and a smoke.)*

*(***BRIAN** *steals* **PATRICK** *away from* **BROOKE** *and, after much prodding, convinces his brother to do shots with him at the bar.)*

(As the band finishes its last tune, **JIMMY** *crosses to the microphone.)*

JIMMY. Alright everyone – last call for the dinner. If you didn't get anything to eat you better come get it now.

*(***TYRONE** *asks* **COLLEEN** *if she would like to get anything to eat. The two cross to the buffet and are the last on line.* **ERIN** *sees the two of them flirting and points this out to anyone who will listen.)*

(As the meal is getting cleared away the band starts to play a specialty song for one of its band members. As soon as the song ends **ERIN** *confronts* **COLLEEN** *at the bar area and the action slowly moves to the center of the dance floor. This escalates into a huge argument. The two sisters lash out at each other and don't hold anything back.* **MAGGIE** *tries to intervene, but is stopped by* **JIMMY***. He escorts her back to her seat.* **ERIN** *lunges at* **COLLEEN** *who at first does not want to stoop to*

ERIN*'s level. When* **ERIN** *takes a second swing at her,* **COLLEEN** *fights back. The girls fight until* **TYRONE** *pulls* **COLLEEN** *off* **ERIN** *and* **BRIAN** *pulls* **ERIN** *off* **COLLEEN**. **PATRICK** *goes to* **COLLEEN** *and pulls her back to his table to assuage the heated situation.)*

*(***BROOKE*** wants nothing to do with this and goes to the ladies room, which does not meet with her approval once she is there. She mistakes one of the mourners for a restroom attendant and complains about the unsanitary conditions and the lack of soft toilet tissue.* **BRIAN** *calms* **ERIN** *down and passes her off to* **JIMMY**. **BRIAN** *asks* **FATHER SEAMUS** *for help as he crosses to the microphone. He gives* **FATHER SEAMUS** *a basket with three potatoes in it.)*

*(***BRIAN*** places the microphone, stand and all, on the dance floor.)*

BRIAN. To honor my father today, I can think of no better way than by playing one of his favorite games. It's called "Pass the Potato." We start off with the potatoes. If you get one, pass it to the guy next to you. When the music stops, one of the three people left holding the potato gets to make a toast to my father. Okay, everyone understand? Let's start.

*(***BRIAN*** strikes up the band and the game starts. Once the potatoes have traveled to a fair number of tables, he cuts off the band from playing. As the first audience members get up to make toasts,* **FATHER SEAMUS** *asks their name and where they are from.* **BRIAN** *repeats this information into the microphone and allows the guests to make their toasts. Afterward* **BRIAN** *cues the band to start the music again. When it stops this time,* **BROOKE LEWIS** *is left holding a potato. She reluctantly crosses to the microphone with* **PATRICK** *leading the way for her. Once* **BROOKE** *is in the spotlight, however she has no intention of leaving.)*

BROOKE. Oh goodness, I'm really not very good at this. I don't know what to say. *(She grabs the microphone.)* I did have the pleasure of meeting Paddy twice over the course of my "eight-year" relationship with Patrick and I found him to be a lovely fellow full of "joi de vivre." And on the positive side, his passing has given us a reason to gather together, and for me to wear this really great Armani Collection suit that just sits in the back of my

*(**BRIAN** grabs the microphone, **BROOKE** grabs it back.)*

I'd also like to say that I thank God for Mr. Finnegan because, after all, if there wasn't a Patrick Finnegan Senior then there wouldn't be a Patrick Finnegan Junior and I'm so lucky to have you, Patrick, and I look forward to spending the rest of my life with you. I love you.

*(**BRIAN** grabs the microphone. **BROOKE** grabs it back.)*

I would like to now sing a song for Paddy

(She sings a verse of a 70s power ballad about crying and keeping it inside.)

*(**BRIAN** grabs microphone once again and she gets it back.)*

In closing, I'd like to share a piece of prose with you that's very dear to my heart. I actually used it as my senior quote in my high school yearbook. It's from the wonderful work "Illusions" by Richard Bach and it goes like this:
"Be not afraid of goodbyes, dear friend, for without goodbyes there can be no…"

*(**BRIAN** grabs the microphone.)*

BRIAN. And goodbye to Brooke Lewis. Okay, let's start the music again.

*(**PATRICK** escorts an annoyed **BROOKE** back to their table. The music starts again and a few more guests*

toast **PADDY** *following the same procedure as before. Then* **TYRONE JEFFERSON** *gets hold of a potato and makes his way up.)*

TYRONE. Paddy was like a father to me at work. He took me under his wing and showed me the ropes. Sometimes after work we would go to one of his pubs for a drink, but sometimes he would come to the other side of town and hang out with me and my buddies. So I dedicate this to him

(He asks **BRIAN** *to join him with a microphone and beat box along in rap fashion.)*

PADDY WAS ALWAYS FULL OF CLASS
HE'D EVEN DRINK HIS BEER FROM A GLASS
SOMETIMES IT'D BE GIN OR SOMETIMES BRANDY
SOMETIMES IT'D BE WHATEVER'S HANDY

(He gets the audience to sing along.)

GO PADDY, GO PADDY, GO PADDY, GO GO
GO PADDY, GO PADDY, GO PADDY, GO GO
PADDY ALWAYS HAD A SMILE ON HIS FACE
HE WAS FULL CHARM, STYLE AND GRACE
WITH A SKIP IN HIS STEP AND A POCKETFUL OF MACE

(He gets the audience to sing along.)

GO PADDY, GO PADDY, GO PADDY, GO GO
GO PADDY, GO PADDY, GO PADDY, GO GO
HE'D CALL ALL THE GIRLS LASSIE
HE'D CALL ALL THE BOYS LADDIE
BUT I'LL ALWAYS REMEMBER HIM
AS MY BLACK IRISH DADDY.

*(***TYRONE*** lifts his drink and looks toward* **MAGGIE,** *then he holds up his fingers in scout fashion and edges back to the crowd.)*

*(***TYRONE*** winks at the crowd. He goes over over to where* **MAGGIE** *is seated and gives her a bear hug.)*

*(BRIAN starts up the band one more time. He is interrupted by **BUSTY QUIVERS**. She crosses to the band and cuts them off, waving her hands in the air.)*

BUSTY. I never got a potato. I'd like to say something too. I, like all of you, loved Paddy very much. We had what you'd call a special friendship.

*(**MAGGIE** stands up and starts to cross to her to stop her from speaking.)*

MAGGIE. This is an outrage! I will not stand for this at my husband's wake! I think I've had enough of these shenanigans!

*(**ERIN** shouts from along side her mother.)*

ERIN. Who is this woman?

*(**ERIN** crosses to **BUSTY** on the dance floor. **MAGGIE** is fuming. **ERIN** brings her to the back of the house by the tables near the bar to calm down.)*

COLLEEN. Hey lady, what's your story?

BUSTY. The name is Busty, Busty Quivers. And if you want to hear my story, listen up sister. When I first met Paddy it was at the *[the name of a local Casino]*. He was sitting at one of those twenty-five cent slot machines. He was wearing his mailman's uniform, he looked so adorable. So I walk over to him and I say, "Hey big boy, is that a roll of quarters in your pocket or are you just happy to see me?" I say that to all the guys. *(She laughs.)* He says, "I don't know the first thing about these machines." I say, "Don't sweat it sweet cheeks, but let's try my machine, it's looser. But first off let me get you a drink." You see, I'm the head cocktail waitress at *[the name of a local Casino]*. So now he's sittin' on my machine. I take his hand and guide his big shiny dollar into my slot. SO I start pulling the handle, real slow at first, 'cause I wanted to savor the fun he was havin'. Then he starts jerkin' it up and down real fast, man o man he was sweatin' bullets. He kept pumping those dollars into my machine. I was pullin', he was pumpin'. Faster and harder, harder and faster. Come on papa, baby needs a new pair of shoes. One cherry... oh oh. Two cherries! oh. Three cherries, yes yes yes ohhh Jackpot!

(**BUSTY** *works herself into a frenzy. She faints and collapses on the floor.*)

FATHER SEAMUS. Is she alright? Okay, everyone calm down. Why don't we take her outside for some air.

(**BRIAN** *and* **JIMMY** *pick* **BUSTY** *up off the floor and carry her off by her hands and feet to the back of the room.* **MAX** *and* **FATHER SEAMUS** *follow behind. After they place her near the ladies room,* **FATHER SEAMUS** *tells the boys that he and* **BILL** *will take care of her.* **PATRICK** *tries to take control of the situation and crosses to the microphone.*)

PATRICK. I think it's time for a little entertainment. What do you say we invite my sister up here to sing a song with me?

(**ERIN** *begins to make her way up to sing with* **PATRICK.**)

My sister Colleen. Hey Colleen come on up here!

(**ERIN** *stops in her tracks when she hears that it is* **COLLEEN** *and not her that* **PATRICK** *wants at the microphone. She retreats to the back by the bar.*)

(**COLLEEN** *makes her way to the dance floor where* **PATRICK** *is. He hands her a microphone.*)

COLLEEN. We're not going to sing "Wild Rover," are we?

PATRICK. Yes. This was our dad's favorite drinking song. We used to sing it at every family gathering. Now we are going to need everyone to clap and stomp along with us when we get to the No Nay Never part ready?

(*They sing "The Wild Rover." As they are singing on the dance floor,* **FATHER SEAMUS** *and* **BILL** *are in the back trying to revive* **BUSTY.** **FATHER SEAMUS** *enters the ladies room asking for some wet towels. They then decide to take her outside to get some air. They are having quite a difficult time trying to stand her up. The two of them* *then try to take her up the entrance-way steps via the pole running down the middle. They are falling over one another and they wind up in some very awkward and compromising positions, sort of like a game of twister without the floor board. Meanwhile back on the dance floor,* **PATRICK** *and* **COLLEEN***, with beers in hand, continue to sing. As they sing the chorus they encourage the audience to sing and clap along.* **KATHERINE** *has given out four tambourines and gives them to four audience members and helps them play along.)*

COLLEEN.

I BEEN A WILD ROVER FOR MANY A YEAR,
AND I'VE SPENT ALL MY MONEY ON WHISKEY AND BEER.
BUT NOW I'M RETURNING WITH GOLD IN GREAT STORE,
AND I NEVER WILL PLAY THE WILD ROVER NO MORE.

PATRICK & COLLEEN.

AND IT'S NO, NAY, NEVER;
NO, NAY, NEVER NO MORE,
WILL I PLAY THE WILD ROVER,
NO NEVER NO MORE.

PATRICK.

I WENT INTO AN ALE HOUSE I USED TO FREQUENT,
AND I TOLD THE LANDLADY MY MONEY WAS SPENT.
I ASKED FOR A BOTTLE; SHE ANSWERED ME "NAY,
SUCH A CUSTOM AS YOURS I CAN GET ANY DAY."

PATRICK & COLLEEN.

AND IT'S NO, NAY, NEVER;
NO, NAY, NEVER NO MORE,
WILL I PLAY THE WILD ROVER,
NO NEVER NO MORE.

COLLEEN.

I'LL GO BACK TO MY PARENTS,
CONFESS WHAT I'VE DONE,

PATRICK.

AND ASK THEM TO PARDON THEIR PRODIGAL SON,

COLLEEN.

AND IF THEY CARESS ME AS OFT TIMES BEFORE,

PATRICK.
> THEN I NEVER WILL PLAY THE WILD ROVER NO MORE.

PATRICK & COLLEEN.
> AND IT'S NO, NAY, NEVER;
> NO, NAY, NEVER NO MORE,
> WILL I PLAY THE WILD ROVER,
> NO NEVER NO MORE.
> AND IT'S NO, NAY, NEVER;
> WILL I PLAY THE WILD ROVER,
> NO NEVER NO MORE.

PATRICK. Let's hear it for my sister Colleen! *(He gives her a hug and a kiss.)* Right now I'd like to ask my beautiful fiancée Brooke Lewis to come up here

BROOKE. Patrick what are you doing? *(joining him on stage)* I'm so embarrassed! Patrick Finnegan sit down right now!

PATRICK. You know Pop was always telling me, "Son, it's time you settle down soon, stop being a wild rover." Well those days are over now, because I have a great job, a wonderful family and finally a woman who makes my life complete, my fiancée Brooke. I'd like to dedicate this song to you. In fact, let's get all the couples up here and join us on the dance floor.

*(**PATRICK** sings a popular love song that the audience can slow dance to. He sings to **BROOKE**. At first she is resists being in front of the crowd, but as the song progresses her icy demeanor melts and she joins in the chorus with him. While **PATRICK** sings to **BROOKE**, **MAGGIE** sits at the table in front of the bar. She looks at all the couples dancing and, for the first time, realizes that she is a widow.)*

*(**JIMMY** and **ERIN** dance with each other, **MAX** dances with a guest and **BILL** and **KATHERINE** dance with each other.)*

*(As **PATRICK** sings, the **BUCKLEYS** start groping each other until **BILL** goes a bit too far and **KATHERINE** drags him off the floor to the back of the bar.)*

(**PATRICK** *finishes singing and kisses* **BROOKE**.)

PATRICK. I love you Brooke.

(**BRIAN** *comes up on the Bandstand and grabs the microphone away from his brother.*)

BRIAN. Now it's a party! Everyone stay on the dance floor because I'm dedicating this next song to my favorite brown-eyed beauty, *[insert audience member's name].*

(**BRIAN** *starts to sing an a party song about his new brown-eyed girl. He sings as if he is at a fraternity house and not very well soon into the song* **PATRICK** *takes over along with* **JIMMY** *and the three form a trio of sorts.*)

(**BRIAN** *shows off some wild moves on the dance floor, moves that only a drunken fraternity boy would do. He gets the whole crowd going.* **TYRONE** *and* **COLLEEN** *grab tambourines and dance together, to* **ERIN**'s *dismay.* **BRIAN** *starts dancing with his brown-eyed girl while* **BUSTY** *dance with a guest. Everyone is having a great time dancing, singing and clapping along.*)

(*Once that song ends the Dublineers play along to two more upbeat modern dance tunes along with a track accompanying.*)

BRIAN. I'd like to get my brother-in-law Jimmy Gilboy up here to sing his famous "Bog Song"! (**BRIAN** *encourages everyone to chant* **JIMMY**'s *name.*) JIMMY! JIMMY! JIMMY! JIMMY! JIMMY!

(**JIMMY** *reluctantly gets up on the Bandstand.*)

JIMMY. All right, all right, I'll sing it. But no shots. You got that Brian?

(*While* **JIMMY** *sings "Bog in the Valley,"* **BRIAN** *goes to the bar and gets a mug of beer and two shots of whisky with the obvious intentions of getting his brother-in-law drunk, he also brings up an audience member to do the shots with him.* **BRIAN** *will encourage the audience to chant Drink, drink, drink at various times during the* *song. When* **JIMMY** *sings the chorus, two of the* **RIVER KIDS** *do a little jig on the dance floor in front of him.)*

JIMMY. *(chorus:)*

YEA, HO!
THE RATTLIN' BOG,
THE BOG DOWN IN THE VALLEY-O.
YEA, HO THE RATTLIN' BOG,
THE BOG DOWN IN THE VALLEY-O.

(repeat chorus as necessary)

NOW IN THAT BOG THERE WAS A ROOT A RARE ROOT,
A RATTLIN' ROOT, ROOT IN THE BOG,
AND THE BOG DOWN IN THE VALLEY-O.

(chorus:)

NOW ON THAT ROOT THERE WAS A TREE,
A RARE TREE, A RATTLIN' TREE.
TREE ON THE ROOT, AND THE ROOT IN THE BOG,
AND BOG DOWN IN THE VALLEY-O.

(chorus:)

NOW ON THAT TREE THERE WAS A LIMB,
A RARE LIMB, A RATTLIN' LIMB.
LIMB ON THE TREE, AND THE TREE ON THE ROOT,
AND THE ROOT IN THE BOG,
AND THE BOG DOWN IN THE VALLEY-O.

(chorus:)

NOW ON THAT LIMB THERE WAS A BRANCH,
A RARE BRANCH, A RATTLIN' BRANCH.
BRANCH ON THE LIMB, AND THE LIMB ON THE TREE,
AND THE TREE ON THE ROOT
AND THE ROOT ON THE BOG,
AND THE BOG DOWN IN THE VALLEY-O.

*(***JIMMY*** does one shot as does the audience member on stage with him.* **BRIAN** *then puts a 'drinking hat' on each of them. A large one on* **JIMMY** *and smaller one on the audience member.)*

(chorus:)

JIMMY. *(cont.)*

NOW ON THAT TWIG THERE WAS A NEST
NOW IN THAT NEST THERE WAS AN EGG

*(***JIMMY*** does the second shot and so does the audience member.)*

NOW IN THAT EGG THERE WAS A BIRD
NOW ON THAT BIRD THERE WAS A FEATHER
NOW ON THAT FEATHER THERE WAS A FLEA,
A RARE FLEA, A RATTLING FLEA

(He pauses and the crowd chants for him to drink. He chugs a full beer until it is empty, the audience member does the same if he or she is so inclined but they have a smaller mug.)

FLEA ON THE FEATHER,
FEATHER ON THE BIRD,
BIRD IN THE EGG,
EGG IN THE NEST,
NEST ON THE TWIG,
TWIG ON THE LIMB,
LIMB ON THE BRANCH,
BRANCH ON THE ROOT,
ROOT IN THE BOG,
AND THE BOG DOWN IN THE VALLEY-O!!!

*(When ***JIMMY*** finishes singing ***BRIAN*** grabs him off the Bandstand and swings him around. ***ERIN*** crosses to the Bandstand and grabs the microphone.)*

BRIAN. Let's hear it for Jimmy and *[audience member]*.

(He grabs the audience member and shouts out his name, and the audience applauds him. He gives him a lottery ticket as a prize.)

ERIN: Alright it's my turn. Daddy would have loved this celebration, so let's keep it going by bringing out my baby Bridget and the River Kids.

*(**ERIN** and the **RIVER KIDS** start to dance. **COLLEEN** crosses to **TYRONE**, who is seated at a table next to the dance floor. She tries to get him to join the dancers. **KEVIN** is getting the audience going by clapping along at various moments.)*

COLLEEN. Come on baby, you can do it.

*(She plants a big wet kiss on his lips. **TYRONE** comes to life. The crowd encourages him to dance. **ERIN** is furious that **COLLEEN** is attempting to upstage her daughter.)*

*(**TYRONE** gives in and starts to tap dance. **ERIN** is mildly amused at **TYRONE**'s abilities, although she is unaware of his talents. **ERIN** tries to show **TYRONE** up in a dance competition.)*

*(**TYRONE** and **ERIN** begin challenging each other with some fancy footwork. It seems that **ERIN** is winning the battle until **TYRONE** decides to join in. **TYRONE** and **ERIN** then begin challenging each other. This time **TYRONE** is winning. **ERIN** decides to sabotage **TYRONE**'s performance by telling the band to stop playing.)*

*(However, it is obvious that **TYRONE** does not need music to dance. This infuriates **ERIN** so much that she runs off the dance floor to enlist the **RIVER KIDS**. She and **KEVIN** gather the troops and deploy a formation of girls upstage while **TYRON** continues dancing. The girls start mocking his performance with hip-hop style gestures. Finally, **ERIN** and the **RIVER KIDS** join forces with **TYRONE** finish with a show-stopping performance featuring a combination of tap and Irish step dancing.)*

FATHER SEAMUS. *(crossing to the microphone on the Bandstand)* Let's hear it for Erin, Tyrone, and the River Kids. They were fantastic!!!

(pause)

Dear family and friends, our guest of honor has arrived. Let us all have a moment of silence for our dearly departed friend Paddy Finnegan.

(We hear the sounds of bagpipes and we see **BILL,** **KATHERINE** *and* **BRIAN** *wheeling* **PADDY***'s corpse in on a hand truck. His hands are crossed over his chest and he is "acting" dead quite brilliantly.* **PADDY** *is fully dressed in his mailman's uniform.* **BRIAN** *wheels him to the coffin and, with the help of* **PATRICK** *and* **JIMMY***, places him into the open casket which* **BILL** *and* **KATHERINE** *have readied for his arrival. Once* **PADDY** *is in the casket,* **MAGGIE** *crosses to look at her husband.)*

(The others take their seats: **MAGGIE, PATRICK, BROOKE, JIMMY, ERIN** *and* **BRIDGET** *are at the Finnegan family table;* **BRIAN** *and* **COLLEEN** *are at the table on the edge of the dance floor where* **BUSTY** *was sitting at the start of ACT II; the others sit at various places around the dance floor, except* **BUSTY** *who stands by the bar.)*

FATHER SEAMUS. Ladies and gentlemen, it is now time to read the last will and testament. I would like to call up the Finnegan family attorney, Max Goldstein.

(As **MAX** *goes up to the microphone on the Bandstand he notices that* **FATHER SEAMUS** *has not adjusted the height. The microphone is way too tall for him, so he has to adjust it himself.* **MAX** *gives* **FATHER SEAMUS** *a look of disapproval. He pulls the will from his pocket, puts on his glasses and begins to read.)*

MAX. Thank you Father Seamus. Remind me when I'm in Israel to have a tree uprooted in your honor. Now this is the time that most of you have been waiting with baited breath and anticipation for I'm going to sing from the Torah – just kidding. We're going to read the will, or as the poor folk say, "Show me the money!" Okay, let's get down to business. *(He burps.)* Excuse me, but the corned beef was definitely not kosher and such small portions. Okay, to all parties concerned, this is my last will and testament dated *[insert date]*. According to the bank President *[insert audience member's name]*, Mr. Finnegan has a net worth of 2.2 million dollars. That's a lot of shekels. To my eldest son Patrick

(**PATRICK** *and* **BROOKE** *stand up.*)

I leave my medals from the Navy, my trusty handgun and the sum of one-hundred thousand dollars.

(*One of the Dublineers is helping* **MAX** *hand out the heirlooms. He gives* **MAX** *each one and in turn* **MAX** *hands them to each family member.*)

BROOKE. That's half our wedding! Oh my God, that's half our wedding!

(**PATRICK** *goes to* **MAX** *to collect his gun, which is in a wooden box and the medals.* **MAX** *hands the box to* **PATRICK**. *He goes back to sit down at the table.*)

(*As each member of the family is mentioned, he or she stands up in place.*)

MAX. Your father would have kvelled for your "Danny Boy." It will always stay with me like the corned beef. To my son Brian, I transfer my beer of the month membership and the sum of one hundred thousand dollars.

(**BRIAN** *crosses to* **MAX** *to get his certificate and then sits back down.*)

BRIAN. Yessss!!!

MAX. To my eldest daughter Erin, I leave one hundred thousand dollars and my dear old mother's brooch for Bridget.

(**ERIN** *crosses to* **MAX**. *As she walks back to her seat she shoots* **COLLEEN** *a look as if to say "sorry you didn't get the brooch."*)

To my youngest daughter Colleen, I hope you forgive me for not understanding. I leave one hundred thousand dollars and my stamp collection. Come on up here you little shichtza.

(**COLLEEN** *is thrilled to have been included and crosses to* **MAX** *to get the collection.*)

To my lovely wife Maggie, I leave you my pension and five hundred thousand dollars. To my friend and co-worker Tyrone Jefferson, I leave you the keys to my Ford Taurus.

TYRONE. Alright!!!

(*He comes up to collect the keys from* **MAX**.)

BRIAN. (*offstage*) Does he get the car too?

MAX. Zoom, zoom.

(*He hands the keys to* **TYRONE**, *who in turn gives him a very elaborate handshake which* **MAX** *shoos away.*)

TYRONE. Alright, I'll be riding in style.

MAX. To Father Seamus and the church, I leave the sum of fifty thousand dollars.

FATHER SEAMUS. Praise be.

(*He turns to an audience member and gives the sign of the cross.*)

MAX. To my cousins Bill and Katherine, I leave one hundred thousand dollars.

(**BILL** *and* **KATHERINE** *hug each other.*)

To my dear, loyal, trusted, tall, good-looking lawyer Max just kidding, I'm not really tall, I leave two hundred and fifty thousand dollars.

(*The family members react with disapproval.*)

Alright, simmer down, simmer down. (*He tries to justify the large amount.*) Legal fees. The remaining one million dollars I leave to my new-found friend, Busty Quivers.

*(We hear a scream from the back of the room. It's **BUSTY**. She runs through the crowd, kissing and hugging guests along the way. She jumps up on the Bandstand and plants a big juicy wet kiss on **MAX**.)*

BUSTY. I'm rich. I'm rich.

*(**MAGGIE** is outraged. She stands up.)*

MAGGIE. That two timing low life drunk, I'll kill him.

*(She crosses upstage to the casket; she is ready to strangle **PADDY**. **MAX** pulls her away.)*

MAX. He's already dead Maggie. It's done. There's nothing you can do about it.

MAGGIE. Oh yes there is. After I get through with him, there'll be nothing left to bury, except his stinking reputation, and that goes for his pig haggis whore too!

*(**BUSTY** crosses to **MAGGIE** and confronts her.)*

BUSTY. I hope you ain't talking about me?

MAGGIE. Oh no. I'm talking about the floozy that's been running around here all day. The one that's been on more "laps" than a napkin.

BUSTY. Lady, I'd put a curse on you, but I see somebody beat me to it!

MAGGIE. Why you little Slut. I'll kill you!

*(**MAGGIE** lunges for **BUSTY**'s throat. She grabs **BUSTY** and throws her to the ground. As they are wrestling. **COLLEEN** and **BRIAN** try to pull them apart.)*

KEVIN. You go girl! Work it out.

TYRONE. My money is on Busty!

*(**PATRICK** and **JIMMY** stand up. Before they even try to break up the fight, **FATHER SEAMUS** runs to the microphone.)*

FATHER SEAMUS. Stop it. Stop it. This is not what Paddy would have wanted.

*(**PADDY** starts to rise out of the casket.)*

PADDY. Get me the hell out of here!

*(Everyone is in total shock. **MAGGIE** faints again. The four Finnegan children rush to help their father out of the casket. **MAX** helps **BUSTY** off the floor and **FATHER SEAMUS** helps **MAGGIE** sit up. **PADDY** tries to stand up straight, he brushes himself off.)*

Boy was I a little stiff.

(He hugs his family.)

BUSTY. Paddy?

PADDY. Busty?

*(**BUSTY** runs into **PADDY**'s arms. She hugs him. **MAGGIE** starts to get up off the floor.)*

MAGGIE. Paddy? What the hell is going on here?

PADDY. Maggie, I swear I can explain everything.

*(**PADDY** pushes **BUSTY** aside. **MAGGIE** gets up off the floor and crosses her arms.)*

MAGGIE. Go ahead. Try me.

PADDY. I never meant to hurt anyone. I was getting sick and tired of everyone constantly bickering about the money. Spend it, do this, do that. I was going nuts. I couldn't take it anymore. So I thought that if I faked my death, it would put an end to it all. Nobody would have to wait for their share of the money. It was crazy, we never should have it Max, Bill, I'm sorry it didn't work out.

MAGGIE. They were in on it too?

PADDY. Yes.

MAGGIE. That imbecile cousin of yours? Why he's a box of rocks.

*(crosses to **BILL** who is on the Bandstand near the casket)*

KATHERINE. Well, so that's why you wanted to embalm him yourself.

*(**KATHERINE** grabs him by the shoulder and drags him off. **MAX** starts to cross downstage when **MAGGIE** turns to him and stops him in his tracks.)*

MAGGIE. Max?

MAX. Maggie, I plead the fifth on this one.

(MAGGIE *turns to* PADDY.)

MAGGIE. You suppose that you could fool your poor wife and everyone else that you was dead as a dog? (*She slaps him across the face.*) You bastard!

(PADDY *is knocked down to the ground.*)

Get up! Get up right now.

(PATRICK *and* BRIAN *help* PADDY *up. He gets off the floor.*)

PADDY. But Maggie

(*She cuts him off.*)

MAGGIE. Shut up. I suppose that you and Miss Big Booty Floozy were going to run off and get married.

(PADDY *is shaking his head "no."*)

Have ten kids and live in a shoe?

PADDY. Maggie please you've got to understand. Nothing ever happened between us. She helped me win the money, that's all. I felt sorry for her. If you really want to know it's you I've always loved.

MAGGIE. Oh really? Well if you really loved me, if you really did, you would've married someone else.

PADDY. Maggie, please?

(MAGGIE *turns and walks back to her table where the gun in the box is placed.*)

MAGGIE. You always have an answer for everything, don't you Patrick Finnegan?

(*She sees the box and the idea of using the gun comes to mind.*)

Paddy, tell me something. When the flag is flying at half mast at the Post Office, what do you think it means?

(**PADDY** *is confused, so he says the first thing that pops into his head.*)

PADDY. They're hiring?

MAGGIE. That's right. And I'm firing.

(*She whips the gun out of the box. She points it at him.* **BRIAN** *rushes up to her and grabs her arm. She swings the gun left then right as* **BRIAN** *leads her arm, everyone pops up and down like doing the wave at a baseball game, without the hands in the air. The gun goes off.* **BUSTY, COLLEEN, BROOKE, TYRONE** *and* **PADDY** *fall to the ground. There is a brief moment of silence.*)

FATHER SEAMUS. Is everyone alright?

(**ERIN** *runs to* **COLLEEN** *and helps her up; it's as if all their problems never existed.* **MAX** *brushes off* **BUSTY**, *including her backside. The last to rise is* **BROOKE** *who is assisted by* **PATRICK**.)

FATHER SEAMUS. Paddy, are you alright?

(**MAGGIE** *runs to* **PADDY** *and helps him get up.*)

PADDY. Yeah, I think so. Woman thank God you're a lousy shot.

MAGGIE. I don't know what came over me. Oh my God, I'm so sorry.

PADDY. Will you ever forgive me for being such an idiot and bringing this whole mess on?

MAGGIE. Paddy what were you thinking? Do you think me that much of a fool?

(**MAGGIE** *gives him a look.*)

PADDY. Only a fool for falling in love with a guy like me.

(*He sings, as the guitarist plays along.*)

I WANDERED TODAY TO THE HILLS MAGGIE
TO WATCH THE SCENE BELOW
THE CREEK AND THE CREAKING OLD MILL MAGGIE
AS WE USED TO LONG LONG AGO.

PADDY. *(cont.)*

> THE GREEN GROVE IS GONE FROM THE HILLS MAGGIE
> WHERE FIRST THE DAISIES SPRUNG
> THE CREALING OLD MILL IS STILL MAGGIE
> SINCE YOU AND I WERE YOUNG
>
> THEY SAY WE HAVE OUTLIVED OUR TIME MAGGIE
> AS DATED AS THE SONG THAT WE HAVE SUNG
> BUT TO ME YOU'RE AS FAIR AS YOU WERE MAGGIE
> WHEN YOU AND I WERE YOUNG
> WHEN YOU AND I WERE YOUNG.

MAGGIE. I do forgive you Patrick Finnegan. I am so sorry. Now do you forgive me for shooting at you?

PADDY. I forgive you but I won't forget.

(She is taken aback.)

MAGGIE. What did you say?

PADDY. Uh, I don't remember. *(He winks at the audience with a glint of Irish mischief.)* I forgot.

MAGGIE. That's why I love you! You old coot, get over here.

PADDY. I'm so sorry. I guess having all that money went to my head. I just want to be a family again, and the only way to do that is… Max give me the will.

*(***MAX*** takes the will out of his pocket and gives it to ***PADDY***)*

Nothing will ever get between the Finnegan's. Not even money!

*(***PADDY*** tears up the will to pieces. He throws them in the air and ***BROOKE*** dives to her knees trying to put it together, ***KATHERINE*** stops her.)*

(They hug and kiss. Everyone cheers them.)

*(***PATRICK*** crosses to ***PADDY***. ***BRIAN*** follows. ***ERIN*** and ***COLLEEN*** stand on the other side of their parents.)*

PATRICK. So Dad, tell us, since you were dead once and you came pretty close just now did you see any white lights at the end of the tunnel?

PADDY. As a matter of fact I did and it was quite depressing.

COLLEEN & ERIN. Why? *(They smile at each other.)*

PADDY. Because I realized that the light at the end of the tunnel was *[local made fun of town]* ! Well, since we're at my wake, why don't we keep the celebration going. I feel like dancing!

*(The band starts to play and **PADDY** breaks into his own style of an Irish jig. **MAGGIE** pulls him away and the **RIVER KIDS** join in. The dance starts with a solo for **BRIDGET**, followed by all the **RIVER KIDS**.)*

*(The entire company joins with a simple Irish step routine. This leads to forming a circle with **PADDY** on the casket in the middle. He is waving to the crowd while taking swings of whisky out of a bottle.)*

*(While **PATRICK** and **BRIAN** spin the casket clockwise, the company circles around him counterclockwise. The boys wheel their father off and join the two parallel lines that have formed for the final moments of the dance. The company ends the dance with their arms in the air and then transition into a company bow.)*

*(**PATRICK** then grabs the microphone and sings one more happy and celebratory pop song as the audience joins in one more time in the dance.)*

The End

CHARACTER BIOGRAPHIES

PADDY FINNEGAN

Patrick James Finnegan was born in County Cork, Ireland. When Paddy was a young boy, his father drowned on a fishing excursion. His mother, Geraldine, then married the town drunk. Between the nightly screams and the occasional beatings young Paddy endured from his evil stepfather, Paddy decided to skip town and head out on his own to America.

Paddy spent his teenage years as a coal miner, a bartender and an amateur boxer. After having almost every bone in his body broken, he gave up on his dream of being the world's greatest prizefighter and got on the next flight to America. While on the flight sitting next to him was a pretty young girl. Her name was Maggie Malone.

This was Paddy and Maggie's first experience flying in a plane. They were both terrified of flying. Paddy proceeded to order a few whiskeys for Maggie and himself. As the flight grew longer, the booze started to slowly take it's effect. As the nerves started to subside, they talked about everything imaginable. They both had dreams of starting a new life in a new country. Halfway through the flight, Maggie was struck by Paddy's charm and quick wit and let him rest his head on her shoulder. He woke up about an hour later, slighty embarrassed about drooling (literally) on his new friend. They shared a laugh and as the plane landed they exchanged addresses and Paddy promised to call on her.

He thanked her for lending her shoulder again, and they went their separate ways. Paddy was off to live with his Uncle and Maggie was off to live with her twin sister.

Paddy moved in with his Uncle Jerry. Jerry Buckley was the brother of Paddy's mother. Jerry had a wife and a son, William. They owned and operated a local Funeral Home, Buckley's Funeral Home. Paddy shared the apartment above the funeral home with his uncle and some other local Irish immigrants. Most of them, like Paddy, dreamed of a better life in the land of opportunity. Paddy's job was to prep and wash the newly arrived stiffs. Paddy had no problems dealing with his new found duties. He would always says, "I ain't afraid of dead people, it's the live ones you've got to be careful about." After a tough day at the "office" Paddy and his buddies would go to the corner Blarney Stone bar. Over many pints of beer and singing some songs along with the jukebox, Paddy would dream of being a rich man in the land of opportunity. But he had no idea yet, how he would attain his wealth. He was just enjoying his freedom in this new land, and meeting new friends.

Paddy enjoyed his nights out with the fellows to share a drink and check out the pretty girls who would drop into O'Leary's Pub.

One night a group of girls came into the pub after working next door in the local department store.

Paddy and his friends bought some drinks for the ladies sitting across the room. After a few bought rounds, the girls invited the boys to join them.

He was introduced to a very pretty girl named Loretta. He immediately took a liking to Loretta, But soon found out that Loretta was married to the local Butcher. Loretta found Paddy charming and cute. She told Paddy about her identical twin sister, her name was Maggie.

Loretta arranged for Paddy and Maggie to go out on a blind date. When Paddy walked into the pub to meet his new date, he couldn't believe his eyes. Lo and behold it was the girl on the flight with him 5 years ago. It was the same Maggie. As Irish luck would have it, they were reunited by destiny. The two picked up where they left off. After a short courtship. Paddy proposed to Maggie and they were married. Maggie moved into the funeral home with Paddy and their other cousins.

While Paddy was working hard in the funeral home, Maggie worked days in the local ice cream store and at nights was busy getting pregnant. Their first was a baby boy they named him Patrick. Three more children would follow – Erin, Colleen and Brian.

Paddy loved to take his family to the beach and to ballgames on the weekends. He is a baseball fanatic. One of the rooms in his home is adorned with Yankee's memorabilia. Paddy also sings in the church Choir and prides himself as a natural.

Although he is slighty tone-deaf, he brings a love of song and Irish charm to every tune.

Paddy is a great storyteller, he is the life of the party, a practical joker, prankster and the first to show up and the last to leave the party. He is not a handy man and the only tool he ever owned is a screwdriver. He knows every bar trick in the world and wins most of his drinks using them. Paddy is not a very religious man, although he is extremely superstitious. He loves to gamble. He plays the lottery religiously and never wins. But he keeps trying his luck. He's a dreamer and sweet kind sould. His key ring consists of many keys, a plastic beer opener and an old worn rabbits foot. He always avoids walking under ladders. And still has a small St. Christopher on his dashboard. The map of Ireland is written all over his face.

MAGGIE FINNEGAN

Born Margaret Mary Malone, ten pounds five ounces in Dublin, Ireland. She was a pretty baby with big blue eyes, a snowy white complexion and apple-shaped cheeks. She was an above average student who enjoyed helping her parents in their bakery shop. She was an expert at wrapping the boxes and making pretty little bows out of string. But this would only hold her interest for so long.

After she graduated from school, she wanted to travel. As a graduation gift, her parents gave her a ticket to America. In the summer of her eighteenth birthday, she left for a better life in America. She found work at the local ice cream store. She maintained her job there until she married Paddy.

Maggie is very dependable, extremely practical and a totally predictable woman. She's not the jealous type, nor is she too easily angered, but be careful if you push her too far – her temper is thunderous. Her one and only obligation is to her family. She takes tremendous pride in being a housewife and mother. She will fight tooth and nail to keep peace among the family.

Every August she looked forward to the annual family vacation to the Poconos. The Finnegans would pack the station wagon with an ice chest filled with beer, soda and Spam sandwiches – Brian's favorite. They'd have more than enough rations to make it to China and back. Maggie would always make sure that their vacation palace had two essentials, a pool for the kids to play in and a bar for Paddy to drink in.

Maggie is not a drinker, but she does like to play bridge, gin rummy and any card game that involves the prospects of winning some money. And when she's not playing bingo at the church she's planning junkets to the local casino.

The apartment is filled with everything Irish, from woolen blankets hand-knit in Dublin to Irish trinkets made of marble. She is a devout Catholic and attends Sunday Mass. Her proudest possessions are a bottle of holy water that she carries around in her purse and a 3D picture of Jesus hanging in her living room. She swears that he's always watching you 'cause his eyes follow you around the room wherever you go. Her home is a little dated, filled with furniture and heirlooms passed down from her dead relatives. But overall, it is impeccably clean, neat and tidy. The sofa and lampshades are all covered with clear plastic. When you arrive at her door she'll greet you with a firm handshake. Then she'll confiscate your coat, briefcase or handbag, hide it in the bedroom and close the door, because she lives by the motto, "There is place for everything and everything in its place." She's the ultimate perfectionist. She works as cafeteria lunch lady.

PATRICK FINNEGAN

Born Patrick David Finnegan in 6 pound 7 ounces. February 26th.

Patrick attended Catholic schools for 12 years of his life. He was a straight-A student. He had a talent for singing in the church choir and was a natural athlete.

He won a baseball scholarship to Georgetown University. An unpredictable knee injury canceled his aspirations of becoming a Yankee first baseman. Patrick put his nose to the books and studied law. In his senior year he landed a job as assistant to the Democratic Senator. While on a summer vacation in Hyanisport, he met his fiancée, Brooke Lewis. Patrick graduated with high honors and was offered a permanent job working for the Democratic Senator. While working in Washington, Patrick applied to join the FBI. He took the test and became a federal agent, which is quite an accomplishment for a Finnegan.

He is the golden child and extremely loyal. Paddy and Maggie manage to take a few days off every year just to visit Patrick. At least twice a year, they drive to D.C. and spend time with their son. Even though his job can be very demanding, he always finds time for his family, whether it is chauffeuring them around town in an "official government vehicle" or just taking them on a sightseeing tour of our county's capital. Patrick, unlike his brother, is highly motivated and well educated. He has come a long way, from playing stickball on the streets of New York to playing politics with the big boys on Capital Hill. Paddy and Maggie are extremely proud of his accomplishments. In their eyes he can do no wrong.

ERIN FINNEGAN

Born Erin Geraldine Finnegan at St. Claire's Hospital. Baby Erin was premature and jaundiced. While the baby spent her first two weeks at the hospital in an incubator, Maggie prayed nightly. She lit votive candles and burned incense. Erin made a speedy and remarkable recovery. According to Maggie it was no less than a miracle. Hence she was dubbed the "MIRACLE BABY."

Erin Finnegan looked like a tiny, fresh-picked strawberry with small tufts of sun-ripened red hair. She was raised watching Sesame Street and could count to ten and sing the theme song when she was only two. If Patrick was a prince, she was more than royalty, she was a goddess.

Every day after work Paddy would come home to his wife and two children and sing "Wait till the sun shines, Nellie." Then Maggie would call them into the kitchen for dinner, which consisted mainly of meat, potatoes and a canned vegetable. Erin was in every school play and dance recital. She was a very gifted child and her parents knew that. Maggie saved everything. It was either pressed into a scrapbook or stuffed into a shoebox stored in the cellar.

During their childhood, Erin and Patrick formed a special bond. Erin idolized her big brother, so much so that she followed right behind him in attending Holy Cross High. Erin dreamed of becoming a ballerina, but instead of ballet, Maggie enrolled her in Irish step dancing classes. In time, the family noticed her potential of becoming a word champion step dancer.

She loved Irish culture, traditions and everything associated with it. Erin's striving for perfection and her desire to live up to her parent's expectations dictated her actions. She was always trying to please everyone. After years of dancing Erin would always come in second place, never coming home with a first-place trophy. Erin felt like a failure and she decided to quit dancing.

To the surprise of her family, she announced that she was going to become a nun. Erin joined the Sisters of Mercy convent. She was overly ambitious and determined to become the best nun the world had ever seen. She always sang the loudest in the choir, added extra Hail Marys to her rosaries, organized bake sales for the homeless and collected the most money for UNICEF. In less than a year the Mother Superior "suggested" that she find other work that suited her "special" personality.

Erin came home and decided to go to college. While earning a degree in teaching at Fordham University she met Jimmy Gilboy. They dated, married and had a daughter named Bridget.

Erin still maintains her close relationship with her older brother Patrick, although she is slightly jealous of his level of success. She works as a teacher. In her free time she trains her daughter in the art of Irish step dancing and has become the quintessential stage mother. You will see her at every one of her daughter's competitions, either shouting from the sidelines or arguing with the judges. Erin is living vicariously through her daughter. The Gilboys live in a perfect little house in a quaint town.

COLLEEN FINNEGAN

Colleen was born the third baby in the family. Everyone was expecting a boy. Paddy even picked out the name Colin. By now the Malone/ Finnegan apartment was overextended. Paddy, Maggie and brood moved to the upstairs apartment.

Baby Colleen was the exact opposite of baby Erin. Colleen was a ten pound package from hell. She never stopped crying or eating. At feeding time Maggie would try to avoid the projectile spoons and forks that baby Colleen would fling across the kitchen. Maggie decided to bring out the big guns and she dusted off the votive candles and prayer cards and, one week later, it was as if the devil himself had exited baby Colleen.

She was the hand-me-down baby. Maggie had saved all of Erin's clothes and had no problem handing them down to Colleen. Unlike her siblings, Colleen was enrolled in a public school; money was just too tight for Paddy and Maggie to send her to a catholic school. While in high school Colleen was an all-star athlete: basketball, softball and field hockey. She was a natural at sports, zippy and fearless. It wasn't until her senior year that she started dating. Colleen went to the senior prom with the star basketball player, Abdul Jamal Hooper. Although her parents didn't approve of their relationship, the two continued to date.

Knowing that no matter how hard she tried he would never be accepted into the Finnegan family, she and Abdul packed their bags and moved to California. She got a job working as a waitress at TGIF. Later that same year, she found out that she was pregnant. When Abdul found this information out, he walked out on Colleen. Knowing full-well that she was not ready to be a single parent and suffering from some medical complications due to the pregnancy, she decided to have an abortion.

Colleen turned to Patrick for help. He wired her the money to help her carry out her wishes. They keep this secret between themselves.

Colleen marches to the tune of a different drummer. Most people think that she's running away from something; she sees it differently. She dreams of climbing Mt. Everest one day. She is single, but dating and works as a barrista at the local Starbucks in San Francisco.

When she isn't working she spends her time studying yoga, Buddhism and holistic medicine.

BRIAN FINNEGAN

Brian, the youngest Finnegan child, was a change of life baby. He was the biggest and most beautiful baby in the maternity ward. Unlike his older siblings, he was a perfect baby. He would sleep through the night without waking and while he was awake he'd always be laughing. He was a little Buddha.

Brian was perfect in every way, until he developed spinal meningitis at the age of five. A long hospital stay and good doctors saved his life. After his recovery Maggie became a little overprotective.

Occasionally Paddy would take him to work with him. He loved to help his father deliver the mail. Paddy would stop by the firehouse on his lunch break and Brian would delight at sliding down the pole or sitting high on top of the hook and ladder truck, where they'd let him honk the horn. The men presented him with a helmet and made him a junior member of the fireman's association. He was only ten at the time. But he knew exactly what he wanted to do with his life. He wanted to be a fireman.

Brian went to a state college. There he became pledge master for Theta Chi fraternity. Brian was not a scholar; in fact, he was almost kicked out of school due to failing grades. What he did posses was a charismatic personality. A great sense of humor and good looks. He was a huge flirt, often juggling many girls at the same time. If he could have installed a revolving door on his dorm room, he would have. In fact he won the Mr. Greek Quad contest during his senior year of college, which only increased his popularity with the women.

After barely graduating college, he returned home to live in the city with his parents. He worked around the corner as bartender in McHales Pub. Working the night shift, he was slinging drinks and burgers to mostly off-duty cops and firemen. Brian enjoyed the perks of the job: free drinks, free food and lots of single girls. But he wanted to fulfill his dream of becoming a fireman.

He took the test and passed it. As soon as he got into the fire academy he quit his job at the bar. He has been on the job for three years now. Brian is still a party animal and a bachelor who has no desire to settle down at the present time. His motto is "Why buy the cow when you can get the milk for free!"

JIMMY AND KEVIN GILBOY

Jimmy Gilboy was a premature baby with the loudest cry and the loudest laugh. Jimmy was red haired, white skinned, a product of his very Irish Catholic Parents. He was a very precocious and curious kid who loved to escape into his room, draw, paint, sing and dance. He played some sports, but his real passion was for the arts. Jimmy was a great student and he joined the school chorus and auditioned for all the musicals. He loved to sing and perform in the local church plays and school musicals. While in 6th grade, Jimmy's mom announced she was pregnant with her second child. She gave birth to a beautiful baby boy. She named him Kevin. Jimmy loved having a little baby brother and would help his mom with raising him. Jimmy would love to sing his brother to sleep and help baby sit. After graduating high school, Jimmy found a job at a local diner as a dishwasher. A few years later Jimmy proved himself to the owner, Gus the Greek and was promoted to manager. Jimmy introduced a very popular karaoke night and it was an instant success.

Jimmy is now the general manager of the tavern.

Jimmy has a huge love of the Irish Culture and is always reading about Celtic lore. He hopes one day to travel to Ireland with Erin to trace his family's history.

Kevin was a very gifted child, but unlike his older brother Jimmy, Kevin had real talent. He won every major dance completion in school and in the local talent shows.

He had a natural gift for movement and dance.

He was a champion Step dancer at age 10. Kevin received a scholarship to College and graduate with a 4.0 degree. He works at the local Irish Step Dancing school and is the head instructor.

He lives alone and he is an avid film buff and theater geek. He is currently dating Charles Santini. Charles is slightly older and currently teaches at the local middle school. They are mostly homebodies and love to travel on their free time. They plan to get married in the future.

BROOKE LEWIS

Born in Westport, Connecticut. She was born a pretty little girl with beautiful blonde hair – a picture-perfect baby. But there was one minor problem; she was born with webbed toes. Her father works as the county judge, while her mother runs her own catering company. Brooke attended a private boarding school for girls in Massachusetts. The Lewis family has descended from a long line of blue blood Presbyterians.

Brooke was the most popular girl in high school. She was a cheerleader, yearbook editor and honor society inductee as well as the captain of her swim team. The girls on her swim team nicknamed her "the duck."

After she graduated from high school her parents gave her money to have corrective surgery on her toes. This put an abrupt end to her swimming career. During the summer months her family would make their annual pilgrimage to their beach house in Hyanisport. During the summer of her senior year of high school, Brooke had a life altering experience – a day on the beach proved to be a date with destiny. While swimming with her girlfriends, Heather and Tiffany, Brooke went out too far and found herself drowning. Not having the advantage of webbed feet, she realized she was in serious trouble. She was a flounder without fins. She was sinking fast.

The lifeguard on duty that summer was a young man named Patrick Finnegan. Upon hearing her cries of despair, he came to her rescue. He dragged her limp and near lifeless body back to shore. He quickly gave her CPR and she miraculously came back to life. Some might say that whole incident was premeditated – perhaps an idea that was hatched from one of those cheap romance novels she secretly read when no one else was watching. She'd spotted her knight in shining armor, actually it was a blue neon Speedo. He was sitting perched in his lifeguard chair, just ripe for the picking. She needed a man in her life and she was determined to get one. Now that she had been accepted to The College of William and Mary in Virginia, having a mate was the next logical order of things. We will never know the truth, but we do know that she's one smart, calculating cookie.

While attending college, Brooke majored in anthropology with a minor in music theory. Patrick and Brooke dated from that summer on. Because Georgetown and William and Mary were only hours apart, it was a short trip to make in her snow-white BMW convertible. Brooke made herself a permanent fixture around the happening Georgetown nightlife. While he was running errands for the senator, she was running formal dances as President of Delta, Delta, Delta sorority. After graduating, Brooke moved to D.C. She currently works as a tour guide with aspirations of becoming the curator for the "Inaugural Ball Gowns of the First Ladies" exhibit at the Smithsonian.

After eight years of dating, Patrick proposed to Brooke. Although no date has been set as yet, Brooke has already picked out the band, dress and is registered all over town at only the finest shops. Someday, Brooke hopes to raise a large family with Patrick and only prays that they might live in a very big house, preferably white, with a rose garden in the backyard. In the meantime, she practices signing her autograph in her daily journal as THE FIRST LADY.

BUSTY QUIVERS

Born Eleanor Quivers somewhere in New Jersey. Her father was an officer in the Navy, and the family found themselves constantly on the move. If they weren't living on the naval base, it was in a small house within a few miles. While Poppa was away, her mom Tootie, entertained gentleman callers. With a fully stocked wet bar, it was an around the clock party at the Quivers household. Many nights while her mom was "entertaining," Eleanor would be alone in her room dreaming of becoming a Hollywood starlet like Ginger or Marilyn. She would sit in front of her mother's vanity mirror rehearsing her acceptance speech at the Oscars.

In between dreams and speeches, she runs errands. She was either picking up groceries or running down to the local 7-11 for beer and ice. Eleanor started hanging out with some of the other navy brats. They were no angels. While mom was away, young Eleanor would invite her friends over to party in her room, smoke pot and drink her mother's booze. And while dad was away mom would play. She'd entertain some of the new recruits on the naval base.

Eleanor's life took on new meaning when she saw saw a movie with a female super hero late one night with. From then on she had a hero. She loved the fact that the female hero could protect the weak, fight evil and destroy men while still being a "Goddess." She wanted to legally change her name to (the hero's name) but her mother wouldn't allow it.

During her rough teenage years, Eleanor matured rapidly in more ways than one. Her chest went from size A to a C in a matter of months. Freddie Rapposelli, her first boyfriend, saw what other boys saw. Thanks to Freddie's special nickname for her, she was now known as "Busty."

Busty was a very popular girl in high school. She graduated with the help of a very satisfied guidance counselor and attended various community colleges, worked part time in a donut shop, and saved enough money to go to flight attendant school. Once she got her wings, Busty started working for a small shuttle company, running a flight from Newark to Atlantic City. It was a short flight, but a few minutes with Busty were all you needed. She was let go when the airline went bankrupt. After that she worked as a cocktail waitress, serving drinks at various dives up and down the Jersey Shore and has picked up a Jersey accent along the way. Each line her face represents a different road traveled and no amount of makeup can cover the rough spots. She currently lives above the Baltimore Grill and works as the head cocktail waitress at the local casino.

FATHER SEAMUS MCMURPHY

Seamus was born in Dublin, Ireland. While his father was reciting Shakespeare as one of the resident actors at the Abbey Theater, his mother stayed home raising the McMurphy kids. Seamus (pronounced SHAY-MUS) was the tenth child of thirteen. He had twelve sisters.

Seamus loved watching his father act. At nineteen he wanted to take a stab at acting. His father was directing the next play; he offered his son a small role that only whet his appetite. He did such a good job that his father gave him a bigger part in the next play. Seamus started dreaming of being a famous actor. Seamus and his father continued performing in plays together for two years. Seamus worked very hard either performing in various plays or working backstage. He loved it all. Working at the theater for three years enabled him to save enough money to travel to England where he was to attend the prestigious Royal Academy. Seamus was not supposed to leave until he finished the last production of the season. The week before graduation, he had a life altering experience.

It was rainy, foggy night. Seamus was walking home with his father after a performance. Three blocks from home a gun-wielding thug approached them. When he demanded money, Seamus dropped to his knees and in a moment of desperation had a quick conversation with God. Suddenly, a bolt of lighting seared through the ominous clouds and struck the gunman down. Seamus, being convinced of the power of prayer, decided at that moment to become a priest. A man of his word, he has never looked back.

BILL & KATHERINE BUCKLEY

Bill was born and raised in New York City. His family runs Buckley's funeral home. The Buckley's are cousins of the Finnegan's. Bill has never been happy working for his family. He has a fear of dead people. When Bill was nineteen he ran away from home. He wound up in Texas working on a cattle farm. But he wasn't happy doing that either. He wanted to be a clown in the circus. One July evening, while attending the circus that was in town, he witnessed a tragic cannon explosion that killed a clown. His aspirations of becoming a circus performer were crushed. Bill returned to work for his family. He sings in the church choir and loves being taken care of by his wife, Katherine. Bill is a very simple man with a heart of gold. His kindness knows no bounds.

Katherine O'Brien was born in Ireland. She came to America when she was twenty. She moved in with her mother's cousin, Jerry Buckley, in New York. She planned to go to school and study marine biology but she didn't have enough money for tuition so she took a job at Buckley's Funeral Home, where she did the make-up and hair for all the corpses. Katherine is a go-getter and she is easily bored with routine. She wanted more, so Katherine got her license and started doing embalming for the company. She still holds the record for the most bodies in one day. After Bill returned from Texas the two met and immediately fell in love even though they were distant cousins. They got married and currently live above the funeral home with their five cats, two dogs and a fish their "children." Katherine wears the pants in the family. In her spare time she loves to garden, preserve and can vegetables, and shoot deer.

MAX GOLDSTEIN

Max Goldstein's father was a deli man and his mother worked in ladies undergarments at the local department store. Max was a quiet kid. Since he was an only child, he spent most of his time in his room with his imaginary friends. Max wanted to be a cowboy. Every Saturday while driving to temple Max would tear off his yarmulke and replace it with a ten-gallon cowboy hat. Max was a puny kid who was constantly badgered for his lunch money. He was the typical nerd all through high school. He played piccolo in his marching band and even made All State. Max is not very athletic, but he did try out for the swim team. When the coach told him he would have to shave the hair off his back, he refused. He told the coach, "I'll sue you and the entire school district for selective discrimination."

Max worked his way through college and law school as the meat man at "Ben's Delicatessen." Max still lives with his mother. He has been dating a nice jewish girl, Rebecca Rosenberg, for the last few years. They met at Weight Watchers. They go on junkets to the local casino every month. He was sitting next to Paddy when he hit the jackpot, Max gave him his card.

TYRONE JEFFERSON

Tyrone lives in a New York City. His parents moved from Detroit and settled in Harlem. Tyrone's father died of a heart attack when he was only two years old. His mother, Florence Jefferson, got a job working as an usher at a local theater. One day she met one of the dancers after the show. His name was Johnny McGuire. After dating for a few months, he moved into her small one-bedroom apartment with Tyrone. Johnny was supposed to go on the road but decided to stay and raise his family. Florence continued working while Johnny became a salesman. Tyrone would often visit their mother and watch the shows from the balcony. He loved dancing and especially tap and free form jazz dancing. Johnny would teach him a few steps when they returned home after the shows. Tyronne met an irish girl while in high school. Her name was Colleen Finnegan. They had a summer romance and she brought him to some of her Irish step dancing school for some lessons. Colleen quickly found out that she wasn't cut out for step dancing. After graduation, Tyronne put his college on hold to support his mom. Florence was ill and Tyronne needed to work any job to support the family. While working in a local restaurant he reunited with his old fling Colleen Finnegan. She suggested he try to apply for a job with the post office. She would talk to her father and try to make things happen. Tyrone passed the postal exam and is currently working as a mailman.

PRODUCTION NOTES

AUDITIONS

In casting *FINNEGAN'S FAREWELL*, it is very important to remember that you need to find an ensemble of actors who can improvise very well. Rather than having them read scenes from the script at auditions, it is better to let them look over the character biographies and give them specific situations for them to improvise. Below are some that we used in casting the original New York company.

BUSTY and **BRIAN**

Busty meets a drunk Brian at the casino and convinces him to go skinny-dipping in the hotel pool.

BUSTY and **ERIN**

Erin is outraged that Busty is at her father's wake and asks her to leave.

PATRICK and **BROOKE**

Brooke is preparing Patrick to meet the Lewis family for the first time at their estate in Connecticut. It will be the social event of the season. He is hung over from a night out with Brian, Jimmy and the boys.

JIMMY and **ERIN**

Erin is outraged that Jimmy not only missed Bridget's dance competition but also forgot to pick up her costume at the cleaners.

ERIN and **COLLEEN**

They see each other for thefirst time infour years and Colleen is out for blood. All their childhood grievances come out.

BRIAN, **PATRICK** and **JIMMY**

Patrick, Brian and Jimmy are at a strip club and Patrick tells his brother that he is going to propose to Brooke, whom Brian never liked.

COLLEEN and **PATRICK**

Colleen tells her brother that she feels like an outsider in his family and is moving away tofind herself.

MAX and **MAGGIE**

Maggie is at Max's office and she finds out that the will is going to be read at Paddy's wake.

MAX and **BILL**

The two are in O'Learys Pub and they reminisce about Paddy. Or they are still in the pub and are fighting as to who will pay for the check. They then realize that they are both broke.

FATHER SEAMUS, MAGGIE and **ERIN**

The three get together to discuss plans for the ceremony for Paddy. Father Seamus has just got back from a Knights of Columbus party where he had too much wine.

TYRONE and **ELTON**

After seeing a picture of Paddy's daughter Colleen, Tyrone and Elton discuss what a fine babe she is. Or Tyrone and Elton try to pick up the same girl at a club.

Two roles that need special attention when casting are Brooke Lewis and Jimmy Gilboy. Both of these actors must understudy three roles each and need to be able to play very diverse characters. In the original concept both of these roles would be cut if they were to go on for one of their covers. However in previews we found that only the character of Brooke can be cut (and Elton, if he goes on for Tyrone). Jimmy has too many responsibilities to be cut completely and therefore needs to be covered by a swing. If Brooke is out the cell phone lines go to Max, her toast gets cut and Patrick sings the ballad to his mother.

The following are suggested understudy breakdowns:

BROOKE LEWIS: Erin Finnegan, Colleen Finnegan, Busty Quivers

JIMMY GILBOY: Patrick Finnegan, Brian Finnegan, Father Seamus

KATHERINE BUCKLEY: Maggie Finnegan

ELTON MCGUIRE: Tyrone Jefferson

Other swings can be brought in to understudy the remaining roles and cover the ones listed above.

Remember this is a unique kind of show, one that allows you to change many aspects of it depending on your location and casting. Don't be afraid to change elements of the show in order to keep the reality. Making these people real and believable is one of the most important aspects in developing the word of the Finnegans. The New York production had the family living in the Hells Kitchen area of NYC, however with some minor changes they can be from anywhere.

Other casting choices may change descriptions. The role of Erin Finnegan should be played by an actress who also can Irish step dance. However this is not a necessity. If Erin can't dance she becomes more of a stage mother, pushing Bridget into being a little star. It is also hard to find an understudy who can Irish step dance and cover Busty Quivers. Remember it is more important to cast a talented actress to play Brooke and cover Erin then another dancer who can only cover Erin. The dance at the end that involves the River Kids, Erin, Tyrone and Elton can also easily be changed if the character of Erin cannot dance; the dance part would then be taken by one of the River Kids. The most important aspect of this dance is that it is a competition between Erin and Colleen, one representing Irish Step and the other Urban Tap.

The character of Bridget; Erin and Jimmy's daughter should be played by a five-year-old Irish Step dancer. However if the youngest available step dancer is older than ten, the character can be changed to a godchild of Erin and Jimmy.

The style of how Patrick sings "Danny Boy" can also be modified depending on the actor playing the role. It is important to utilize the actor's strongest vocal qualities and use them. In the New York company various actors have played Patrick, and each time it was changed to suit the actor, without taking anything away from the moment. He has sung the second verse of the song with a rock, R&B, or a Broadway flair; each one has worked in its own way. There is no right or wrong, as long as it starts sincere, very straight and legit and builds to something way over the top and inappropriate at a funeral. Remember that Patrick is not "performing" for anyone, the moment needs to consume him in whatever way works best for the actor.

REHEARSALS

The rehearsal process for *FINNEGAN'S FAREWELL* is very unique since so many of the moments in the show are created between the actors and the audience. Therefore it is important to stress, do not over rehearse the show, after a while actors will start talking to empty chairs. After the entire play is blocked and staged, and everyone feels comfortable with the whole history of each character, bring in some sort of an audience and let the actors experiment. This is the only way the show can grow. In the New York production we had a long preview process to allow the actors to figure out all their business.

Break down your rehearsals into four sections:

1. The Church

2. The Party

3. The Dance and Musical Numbers

4. Family History and Biographies

The family history and biographies are some of the most important and informative rehearsals that will occur. Besides the biographies provided in the script, each actor should write out a biography and make sure everyone in the cast has access to it. The stage manager should keep a "Family Album" with everyone's bio in it. These biographies should have specific facts about each character that may come up in the course of an improvisation during the show. It also makes for a fuller and more complete character. Remember the actor's choices should be real and not contradict any of the given circumstance that is already a part of the play. Some characters may or may not know some of this information, but the actors should be aware of everyone's complete life story and storyline. For example one good question would be "How did Patrick propose to

Brooke?" There should be one answer to this question, but not every character should or would know the answer to it. Characters should also figure out if they are meeting each other for the first time at the wake. No one other than Bill and Max should know Busty Quivers.

During rehearsals the company needs to agree that no matter what the circumstances are, that they never break character. After a while the actors will learn to speak to each other in code to communicate thoughts without breaking. It is also important to remember this is the funeral of Paddy Finnegan not a "show". Audience members will ask questions that everyone should be prepared for, even before the first preview. They will ask questions ranging from, "What do you do with the casket when it rains for a show?" to "How many days do you have to eat corned beef and cabbage?" For the most part the audience member is just curious and not trying to throw you off. As long as everyone knows their character inside and out, they can and will answer any question that is posed to them. This also needs to be true for the dancers and the band. Although most questions will be addressed to the actors, the Dublineers and the River Kids must be told that the reality of the show must be maintained at all times.

It is also important that the actors remember each of their character relationship to each other. It is especially difficult in an interactive show when actors become too casual and friendly with each other and forget the characters relationships. Certain characters would never start a conversation with other characters in this show. For example Erin would not enter a casual conversation with Busty or Brooke, unless there was some ulterior motive for Erin.

The church and Vinnie Blacks Coliseum were down the treet from each other in the NY production. However if only one space is available this can be easily changed by having the service at the catering hall. However, if a procession from one place to another is happening (which really adds a nice touch to the show), it is important that the procession down the street be staged like the rest of the show. The order of the procession can vary, however it is important to space the actors out to take care of groups of the audience. This is necessary not only for entertainment value, but also for safety. Remember Brian is in a uniform and can stop traffic just as easy as any cop on the street. Besides it is not everyday that people can see a casket rolling down a busy avenue. The bagpiper should be in the front of the procession with the casket close behind and Max should bring up the rear holding the flower arrangement. This allows onlookers a distinct visual of just how long the procession is.

THE RUNNING OF THE SHOW

The audience can sometimes get a bit out of hand at an interactive show. Remember there is a cash bar and sometimes groups come after they have had a few drinks already. At one performance in NYC, one man stormed to the casket and was screaming how Paddy was his father also. When these situations arise the actors must stay in character, in the "world of the wake" and deal with the circumstances as best they can. Being as Jimmy Gilboy is the manager of Vinnie's he took it upon himself to escort the gentleman out with some help from Brian. The Stage Managers should be ready to deal with these situations and should go over a game plan with the actors should these problems arise in advance.

One area of the show that allows the audience to really participate and get involved is "Pass the Potato". The actors playing Brian and Father Seamus really need to take control of this section and keep the pace moving. If someone seems like they are going to go overboard, the actors have the power to stop them before they reach the microphone. Father Seamus should ask everyone their name and where they are from so Brian can repeat it. He can make each audience member feel like they are part of the Finnegan family. Brian also needs to be able to cut anyone off who goes on a bit too long. No toast/speech should last more than a minute. The actors playing Brooke and Tyrone have the freedom to change their speech/rap depending on the night. They can incorporate an audience member that they have met during the show, or add some bit of news events to keep the show very current.

Speaking of microphones and speeches...whenever anyone is on the mic *all* focus must be paid to them. If everyone in the cast is not focusing on the action on the "stage" how can it be expected that the audience will be paying attention to them. This also holds true for the River Kids dance numbers. It is all right to comment on the action, but do not take away focus from it by engaging an audience member or other character in an improvisation. There is plenty of time duringdinner for that.

In order for *Finnegan's Farewell* to work it takes a group of dedicated and intelligent actors, dancers and musicians. Everyone must work together as a team if the audience is to feel that they are meeting real people who knew Paddy Finnegan. The whole show is performed all around them, creating one of the most complete theatrical experiences one could have. Some of the most touching and wonderful moments in this show are the little personal encounters between a character and audience member or two characters having a scene in a remote area of the playing space. Although only a few audience members get to see and appreciate these exchanges, don't negate how important they are to the show as a whole.

For the two hour running time of the show the actors must remember that they are these characters; all of their personal issues should be left in the dressing room. It actually is a wonderful experience for an actor to become someone else for a few hours, not having time to think of his or her own lives for a while. Every show should be looked at as a new learning experience, a challenge for every actor in the cast to develop their skills. The more immersed they are in the characters lives, the more real the show is, and the more fulfilling the experience will be not only for the audience but for the company as well.

PROPERTIES LIST

SERVICE: *(Preset)*

Casket, traditional wood with two handles on each side

Casket stand on wheels with green drape covering it

Green carnation flower arrangement in the shape of a shamrock

Podium

Two three-foot high candleholders

Two table top candleholders

Four white candles (can be electric)

Three-foot by one-foot altar table with purple drape

Four armbands for the pallbearers

Various framed pictures of the Finnegan family, including one sports shot of Brian, Brooke and Patrick's engagement shot and one of Paddy taken a few weeks ago

A long flower arrangement for on top of the casket with flowers of the season

Various mass cards Reserved signs

SERVICE: *(Personal)*

Father Seamus: Bible

Brian Finnegan: Cigarettes and lighter

Brooke Lewis: Handbag with working cell phone, mints, lipstick and compact

Maggie Finnegan: Black purse with tissues, pictures of Bridget and various prayer cards

Patrick Finnegan: Cell phone

Colleen Finnegan: Very beat up and worn red backpack on wheels, filled with clothes

Max Goldstein: Old tan briefcase with the will, legal documents and business cards

Bill Buckley: Business cards

Busty Quivers: A zebra handbag with tissues, wrapped sour balls, cigarettes, matches from various casinos in Atlantic City, transit bus schedule, makeup, nail polish, nail file, pills, chewing gum, perfume (something cheap), small spritz bottle of Aqua Net, brush, pick, old keno tickets and dice

Altar Girls: Two prayer candles

CATERING HALL: *(Preset)*

Fifteen Bottles of beer (brown) filled with water 4 Shot glasses

One Whiskey bottle filled with iced tea

Two 'drinking' hats

Plastic vase with green carnation on each table

Irish flag over the Bandstand 4 potatoes in a wicker basket
Starter pistol in a wooden box
Blank bullets
Antique brooch in a felt case
Stamp collection in plaid photo album
Beer of the month club framed certificate
Car keys on a tacky key chain
Two tambourines
Tray with a mug filled with (non alcoholic) beer
Handcart

CATERING HALL: *(Personal)*
Brooke: a champagne flute filled with ginger ale
Katherine: a casket catalogue
Bridget: a trophy from her last dance competition
Max: Last will and testament

COSTUMES

PADDY FINNEGAN:
Postal shirt Postal pants
Postal sweater Postal tie
Postal hat (baseball style) Black shoes
Black socks Black belt

BRIAN FINNEGAN:
Full dress fireman's uniform (with appropriate patches)
Tie
Jacket
Pants
Black belt
Shirt (with appropriate patches)
Fireman's badge (with black mourning band over numbers)
Fireman's hat (with either Maltese cross or other appropriate ornament)
White stretch cotton gloves
Navy full-length topcoat (if necessary)
Black patent leather shoes
Black socks

PATRICK FINNEGAN:
Black conservative suit
White shirt with collar that snaps under the tie

Black belt
Black shoes
Black socks
Tie with muted green colors
Formal topcoat (if necessary)

JIMMY GILBOY:
Green plaid jacket White or cream shirt
Vest that coordinates with jacket
Khaki colored pants
Green stripe tie
Brown belt
Brown shoes
Brown socks
Cladder wedding ring
Casual topcoat (if necessary)

MAX GOLDSTEIN:
Gray pinstripe suit (very conservative)
Burgundy stripe white shirt
Coordinated bow tie (not pre-tied)
Coordinated suspenders
Black wing-tip shoes
Dark gray socks
Conservative style topcoat (if necessary)

FATHER SEAMUS:
Black suit
Black priest shirt with white plastic collar insert
Black shoes Black belt
Various religious pins (i.e. cross) on jacket lapel
Black socks
Religious stole for church ceremony

BILL BUCKLEY:
Navy three- piece suit (too small)
Blue shirt
Loud tie Black shoes Black belt
Black socks
Old topcoat (if necessary)

TYRONE JEFFERSON :
Postal shirt

Local basketball team playing jersey personalized with Tyrone's last
    name (worn inderneath)
Postal pants
Postal sweater
Postal tie
Postal hat (baseball style)
Black sneakers
Black socks
Black belt
Postal style chain with route mailbox keys on it that is attached to belt
Casual topcoat (Postal if possible)
Black tap shoes

MAGGIE FINNEGAN:
Two piece black dress (black dress with matching black jacket)
Black simple shoes
Black panty hose
Black dance briefs
Black pillbox style hat with whimsy
Black handbag
Jewelry with green accents, small shamrock pin or guardian angel pin
Simple black or green outdoor coat (if necessary)
Cladder wedding ring

KATHERINE BUCKLEY:
Black blouse with high neck Black straight skirt
Black hose
Black shoes (Oxford style)
Black or muted color outdoor coat (if necessary)
Wedding ring

BUSTY QUIVERS:
Very tight black dress made of stretch material with zebra trim and
    lots of cleavage
Very high heels made silver and black zebra pattern
Black lace pantyhose
Black dance briefs
Frosted blond wig
Padded bra (if necessary)
"Dice" earrings
Double strand large pearl choker
"Glamour length" fingernails or black net/lace gloves
Large brimmed, black hat with white feather and black whimsy

Black and white fake zebra outdoor coat (if necessary) Large black zebra print handbag

Large sunglasses

COLLEEN FINNEGAN:

Very wrinkled tie-dyed royal blue "India" style skirt (drawstring waist)

Red stretch top

Black macrame vest (to hips)

Brown ankle walking boots Cream tights

Wrist/ankle "India" style bracelets that "tinkle"

Various beaded necklaces, chokers Celtic symbol earrings

Multi-colored southwest American Indian style coat (if necessary)

ERIN FINNEGAN:

Green blazer

Green plaid skirt

Navy blue blouse

Black sweater

Patent leather "Mary-Jane's"

Black tights

Black dance pants

Cross necklace

Cladder wedding ring

Small black handbag

Simple outdoor coat (if necessary)

BROOKE LEWIS:

Conservative/trendy, expensive burgundy suit Black, expensive/trendy shoes

Fake "Prada" bag

Nude pantyhose

2 carat diamond ring

Pearl necklace and earrings

Simple, expensive coat in dark color

BRIDGET GILBOY:

Plaid skirt

White blouse

Navy blue sweater

Black Mary-Jane's

Black tights

Little girl's dress coat

Also: Irish dance costume

KEVIN GILBOY:
    Black dance pants
    Black silk shirt (service)
    Green silk shirt (party)
    Dance shoes
RIVER KIDS:
    Irish dance costumes
    Black soft shoes
    Black hard shoes

IRISH BAND MEMBERS:
    Green vest (with Dublineers embroidered left/front)
    Black pants
    White shirt
    Black shoes
    Black socks

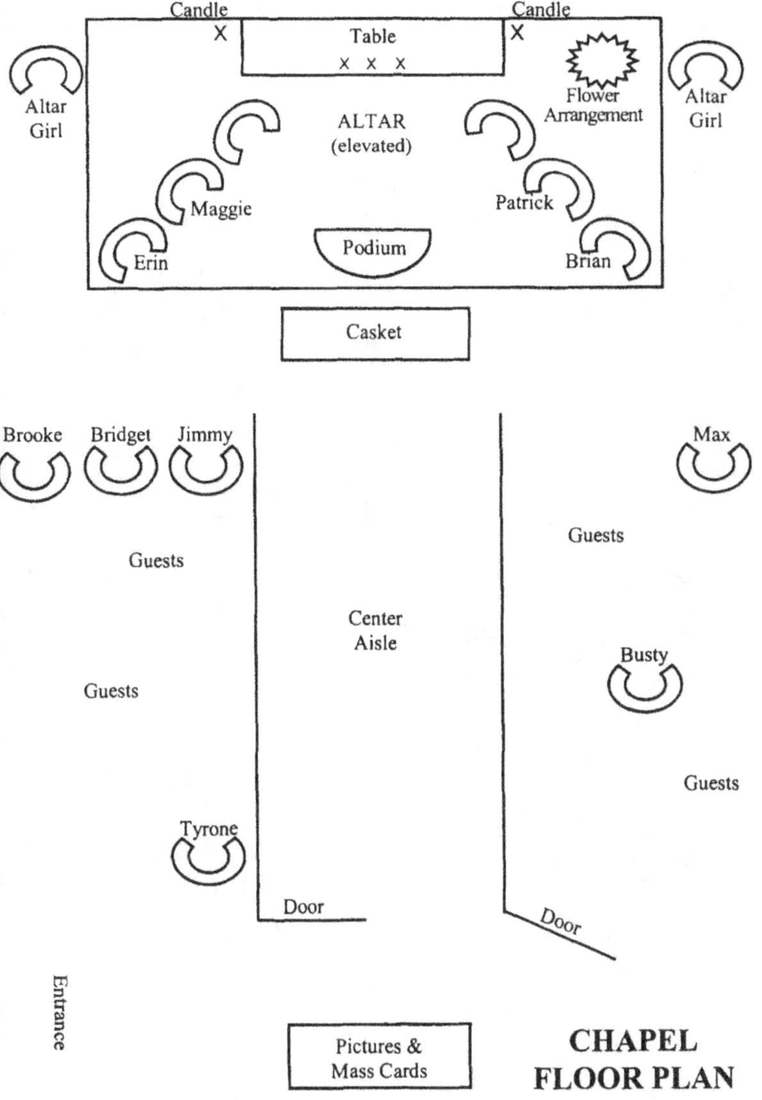

Candle
X
Candle
X
Table
X X X
Altar
Girl
ALTAR
(elevated)
Flower
Arrangement
Altar
Girl
Maggie
Patrick
Erin
Podium
Brian
Casket
Brooke
Bridget
Jimmy
Max
Guests
Guests
Center
Aisle
Busty
Guests
Guests
Tyrone
Door
Door
Entrance
Pictures &
Mass Cards
CHAPEL
FLOOR PLAN

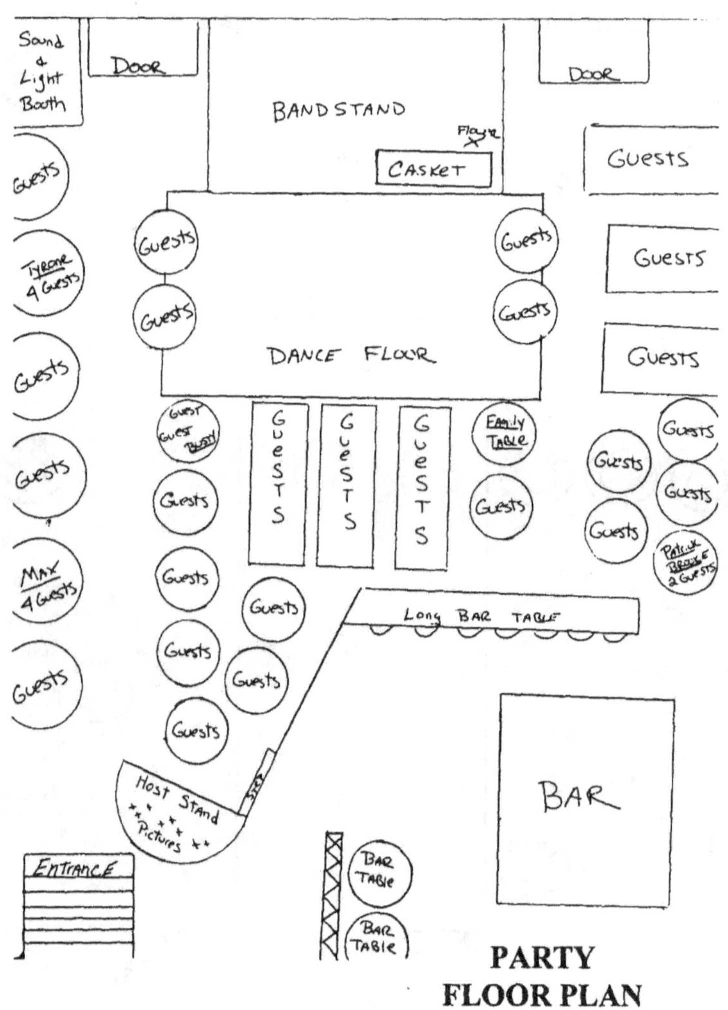

PARTY FLOOR PLAN